Keeping Secrets at Dark Creek

NIKKI TATE

Keeping Secrets at Dark Creek

NIKKI TATE

VICTORIA, BRITISH COLUMBIA

National Library of Canada Cataloguing in Publication Data

Tate, Nikki, 1962-
    Keeping secrets at Dark Creek

    (StableMates ; #7)
    ISBN 1-55039-123-2
I. Title. II. Series.
PS8589.A8735K43 2002   jC813'.54   C2001-911743-4
PZ7.T2113Ke 2002

Sono Nis Press gratefully acknowledges the support for our publishing program provided by the Government of Canada through the Book Publishing Industry Development Program (BPIDP), the Canada Council for the Arts, and the British Columbia Arts Council.

Cover illustration by Pat Cupples
Map by E. Colin Williams
Cover design by Jim Brennan

Published by
Sono Nis Press
PO Box 5550, Stn. B
Victoria, BC V8R 6S4
1-800-370-5228

Distributed in the U.S. by
Orca Book Publishers
Box 468
Custer, WA 98240-0468
1-800-210-5277

sononis@islandnet.com
www.islandnet.com/sononis/

PRINTED AND BOUND IN CANADA BY FRIESENS PRINTING.

Interior artwork *Face to Face* by:
Joan Larson CREEKSIDE STUDIO
(250) 752-0395
www.joanlarson.com

For M.C. & P.H.—
who dared to dream

With thanks to Brian,
who can spot the difference between
an Elgin and a Waltham at fifty paces

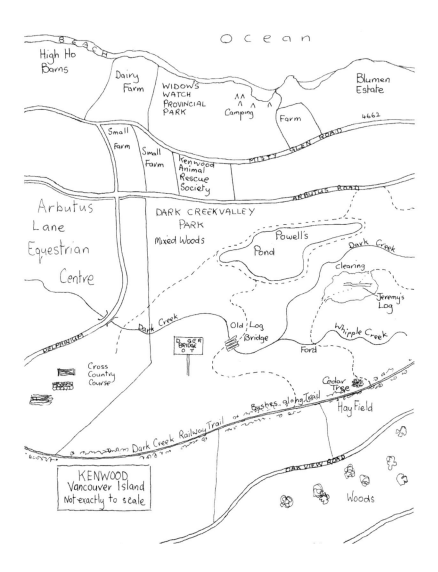

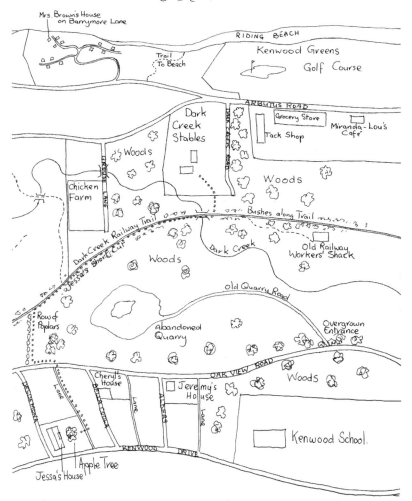

1

Jessa jumped. "Don't sneak up on me like that!"

Cheryl Waters dropped her books on the floor with a loud thwack, making Jessa jump again. "A little nervous, are we?"

"I hate these locks."

Combination locks were one of about a thousand things that were different and unpleasant about Kenwood Middle School.

"What class do you have next?"

"I don't know. My schedule is taped up in there." Jessa banged her locker door and started twiddling the lock again.

"Didn't you listen to Mr. Belwell in the assembly this morning?"

"Cheryl, stop talking to me or I'll never get my lock open." Jessa rolled her eyes and kept working her lock. The principal had droned on and on and on about various items on the cafeteria menu, how great the sports teams were at Kenwood Middle School, and how much he loved it when students made posters for the School Spirit bulletin board just inside the front doors of the school.

He'd also suggested that students keep their schedules in their backpacks, an idea Jessa had thought was a bit silly. At Kenwood Elementary she had never forgotten where she was going next.

". . . now past the zero to number twenty and . . ."

Bang! Jessa smacked the locker door again. Cheryl suddenly looked concerned.

"Are you okay? Are you low or something?"

Jessa spun around to face her friend. "I am perfectly fine. And what did I tell you about mentioning—that?"

"What, your diabetes?"

"Shhh!"

"Calm down! I was just worried—"

"There's nothing to be worried about. I have a juice in my backpack in case I need it. There is no reason for all these kids to know. . . ."

Cheryl pushed out her bottom lip in an exaggerated pout. "I wasn't telling the whole world. I was just checking to make sure you were okay. Excuse me for living."

For a moment the two girls stared at each other and then Jessa looked down at her hands. "I'm sorry. It's just—I don't like this school. Too many dumb . . ." Jessa groped for the word Mr. Belwell had used in that morning's assembly.

"Initiatives?" Cheryl offered.

"Yeah. Initiatives. Like that stupid School Spirit bulletin board."

"What's wrong with that? I think it's a good idea—I can see my picture up there now. Can't you just see the head-lines? 'K.M.S. Student Discovered by Hollywood Producer'!"

"Oh, please. Spare me. Obviously he meant real kids doing real stuff."

Cheryl slumped against the locker next to Jessa's. "You're right. We should make a poster to celebrate your lock-opening skills."

"You are soooo helpful." Jessa glared at her lock as if she could melt it right off her locker door.

"Do you want me to try getting your lock open? We're already late. We'll get expelled if you don't break in there soon."

Jessa looked along the hallway. It was nearly empty except for a few other lost-looking seventh graders.

"Fine." She stepped out of the way and told Cheryl her combination.

Cheryl twiddled the knob right, left, then right again.

"Thank you," Jessa said as her locker door swung open. She glanced at the schedule on the inside of the door. "Oh, great. English. What do you have?"

"Draaaahmaaaah, dahling."

Jessa laughed in spite of herself. Cheryl's face was contorted into a caricature of a beauty queen complete with rosebud lips and fluttering eyelashes.

"Meet you at lunch?"

"Why, certainly, dahling. We can talk over macaroni and cheese a la carte. Ta-ta—must run. Mustn't keep my adoring public waiting."

Jessa closed her locker and turned around, trying to get her bearings. Kenwood Middle School was just way too big. She would never get used to it. Never.

". . . regular written assignments and two memorized pieces of poetry to be presented to the class each term. I expect you all . . ."

The teacher stopped talking as Jessa opened the door. Everyone in the class watched as she found a seat towards the back.

Mr. Small. The teacher's name was printed in tidy writing on the board at the front of the classroom. Jessa ducked her head down and rooted through her backpack for paper and pencil so Mr. Small couldn't see her smiling. The teacher didn't fit his name at all—he was anything but small. He wasn't exactly fat, but he was huge—so tall that Jessa wondered whether he had to duck to clear the door jamb without hitting his head.

"Good morning, Miss? . . ."

"Richardson. Jessa Richardson."

Jessa's cheeks burned. Why had she been late on her first day? She glanced around the classroom, looking for a sympathetic face. At least half the kids she had never seen before. She caught a glimpse of Midori and Rachel, friends she knew from Grade Six at Kenwood Elementary. Midori bobbed her head ever so slightly and Jessa felt a little less alone. But only for a moment.

"As I was saying, I expect you all to hand your assignments in promptly and to be prepared when you come to class. I shouldn't need to add that I expect you all to be on time."

A couple of kids behind Jessa stifled snickers.

"Miss Richardson—Jessa. Would you please come up to the front. . . ."

For one dreadful moment Jessa thought he was going to punish her in front of the class, or make her tell everyone what she had done over the summer vacation, or . . . She felt quite faint and reached out to touch her desk to steady herself.

". . . to pick up your textbook. Sign the sheet on my desk and—"

Just then the door opened a crack and a boy poked his head in. Another kid who hadn't attended Kenwood Elementary. There were lots of new faces this year. Jessa took advantage of the distraction and slipped up to the front to get her book.

Mr. Small sighed. "Good morning, Mr.? . . ."

"Timmins." The boy's face turned bright scarlet

beneath his close-cropped white-blond hair. He froze in the doorway.

"Do you have a first name, Mr. Timmins?"

"Yes, sir."

Two boys over by the window giggled.

"Would you like to tell us your name?"

"Oh. Andrew. Andrew Timmins."

"Very good. Welcome to English Seven. My name is Mr. Small." He nodded towards the blackboard.

The boy found an empty seat in the row next to Jessa's. He tucked his bookbag under the desk and sat awkwardly on the edge of his seat, trying not to look at anyone. Jessa couldn't believe anyone could be even more uncomfortable than she was, but Andrew Timmins looked as if he would rather be anywhere else than in his desk.

He, too, was summoned to the front of the class to pick up his textbook and sign for it. Once back at his desk he flipped through the book, his knee constantly jiggling up and down. He flicked his pen against his thigh and squirmed and wiggled so much, Jessa could hardly pay attention to a word Mr. Small said. She decided that next time she would arrive early for English class so she could sit as far away from Mr. Andrew Timmins as possible.

Mr. Small spent most of the class describing what everyone could expect for the coming year. At the end of the class he added, "Please take note of where you are sitting. That will be your assigned seat, at least until I know all your names. Enjoy the rest of your day!"

Jessa slumped back into her chair. There wasn't much chance she'd enjoy anything at this stupid school. The bell rang and the students rose with noisy shouts and laughter and headed for the door. Jessa bit her bottom lip as she realized she still had no idea where she was going next. In her rush she had left her dumb schedule taped up inside her locker.

2

"So, how was your morning?" Cheryl seemed disgustingly cheerful.

"Guess."

"That good, huh?"

"Do you have Mr. Small for English?" Jessa asked.

"Nope. Ms. Elliot. She's really cool. She went to Nepal this summer. She spent the whole class telling us about this zoo she visited in Patan. You know what she did while she was there?"

Jessa shrugged. "Fed the ducks?"

Cheryl's eyes grew wide and she leaned closer. "She had her palm read. I bet she's going to be reincarnated as a wise old elephant."

Jessa pushed her shepherd's pie around her plate as Cheryl chattered on about her wonderful classes and interesting teachers.

"This is awful," Jessa complained.

"I don't know—it's more sophisticated than macaroni and cheese, don't you think? I mean, macaroni and cheese is fine for little kids—they won't eat anything more adventurous. Try ketchup."

That was Cheryl's solution for every questionable dish.

"Disgusting," Jessa said.

"So don't eat."

Jessa scowled. "I have to eat. You know that. I had my shot this morning." Jessa smashed the meat and gravy into the soft potatoes with her fork. She had been diagnosed with diabetes just that summer, and she still wasn't completely used to having insulin shots morning and night and having to eat certain amounts at set times during the day. She could hardly blame Cheryl for forgetting.

"Oh, right. Well, eat something else."

"I don't have any more money. Never mind. I'll eat it." She picked up a forkful of brown mush and pinched her nose shut. Maybe a bit of ketchup wasn't such a bad idea.

"Are you going to the barn after school?"

For the first time all day, Jessa grinned.

"For sure. I have a lesson on Jasmine and then I'm doing evening feed. Are you riding?"

Cheryl nodded. "I'm going right after school. Do you want to get a ride with me?"

"Sure. I'll call my mom and let her know. She can probably drive you home."

"Sounds like a plan to me. My trusty steed, Billy Jack, awaits!"

Jessa laughed and the sound surprised her. Being happy was easy, she decided. All she had to do was keep her mind on the barn and nothing else really mattered.

"Slow down! You're going to . . ."

Jessa didn't hear the rest of whatever Mrs. Bailey was about to say because Jasmine launched herself from a stride and a half out and jumped huge. The unexpected thrust catapulted Jessa forward and as they landed on the other side of the little oxer, Jessa found herself sprawled over Jasmine's neck.

"Sit up!"

Right. That was easy for Mrs. Bailey to say! One . . . two . . . three . . . Automatically, Jessa counted strides between the fences even though she was so far out of position. The line called for six easy strides, but if Jasmine jumped with Jessa hanging on like a desperate monkey, she would come off for sure.

Somehow, Jessa managed to push herself back into the saddle, but as they approached the next fence, a small vertical, her left foot slipped from the stirrup. Without urging, Jasmine leaped over the jump, pulling the reins through Jessa's fingers.

"Sit up! Get back into position—circle! Take a circle. Come back to trot! Pick up your reins—they're flapping every which way!"

Mrs. Bailey shouted a string of instructions at Jessa, who said "Whoa" in her most assertive voice. Jasmine dropped to a rollicking trot, rather excited after the quick line.

"And walk now—give her a loose rein."

Jessa did as she was told, found her dropped stirrup, and looked out across the field behind the riding ring. Brandy and Sienna stood head to head, snoozing in the late afternoon sunshine. Cheryl and Billy Jack rode slow, relaxed circles out in the field.

"Stop daydreaming and come here. That was terrible! Tell me what went wrong."

"We were too fast coming into the line and she jumped huge. . . ."

"And why did she do that?"

"I'm not sure."

"You know she could easily have added another stride in there. Why did she take off where she did?"

"I'm not sure. . . . I didn't want her to."

"You may not have wanted her to, but you did ask her to jump."

Jessa knew better than to argue, but she was sure she hadn't asked the big mare to take off where she had. Jasmine had dreamed up that little trick all by herself.

"You threw your body forward when you saw the jump coming at you."

"I did?"

"You certainly did. And Jasmine did exactly what she thought you wanted—she jumped. You are very lucky she is such a good girl. Another horse might have run out between the fences, what with you sprawling all over the place up there. She had the good sense to keep going, though I didn't think you'd stick with her. Now why the tears?"

Why did she think? Riding Jasmine was horrible. Rebel never did stupid things like launch himself into the air from six kilometres before the fence.

"Jessa. You did a fine job staying on, all things considered. The good things were that you didn't catch her in the mouth, you managed to get over the second jump, and, I think, you learned something. You wouldn't learn much if you did it all perfectly the first time, would you? Now, you'd better try that again. This time, ride in slooooowly."

Jessa sniffled and wiped her nose with the back of her hand.

"They are tiny jumps—not even up to Jasmine's knees. She could step over these backwards! Your job is to concentrate on getting a nice steady canter, to bring her to the first fence nice and straight. Remember, wait for the jump to come to you. There is no rush."

Jasmine snorted and Jessa jumped. The humiliation made her start crying all over again. She felt like such a baby.

"Jessa—take a minute to pull yourself together. Molly? Are you ready?"

It was all Jessa could do not to tip her head back and wail like a wounded wolf. Not only was she having a terrible riding lesson, Molly was there, too, to witness all her zillions of mistakes.

"Sure." Molly grinned, gathered up Rebel's reins, and picked up a steady canter. Of course, Rebel picked up the correct lead the first time, unlike Jasmine, who seemed to be pretending she couldn't tell her left from right.

Off they went, girl and pony, a perfect little team approaching the first of several jumps in the mini-course Mrs. Bailey had set up. The jumps were set so low Rebel managed them without any trouble at all. He wasn't allowed to jump more than once a week and then over only the smallest of fences. He was getting on in years and Mrs. Bailey said it was important to baby him a bit so he'd be sound for a long time to come.

After easily navigating two sets of cross-poles set three strides apart, Rebel pricked his ears towards the tiny oxer that had caused Jessa and Jasmine so much grief.

"One . . . two . . . three . . ." Jessa counted under her breath. Rebel found the perfect distance and then cantered through the line getting the seven forward strides he needed for a smooth ride. As Molly and Rebel hopped over the next fence, Molly's long, brown ponytail bounced against her back.

Molly brought Rebel back to a trot, circled once, and then halted.

"Very nice, Molly. I'd like to see a longer release—you didn't catch him in the mouth, but if you had been any less balanced and organized up there, you didn't give yourself much room for error. We have to look after this old boy, right, Rebel?"

Jessa bristled. Rebel was such a great pony. She hated it that these days she had to ride Jasmine nearly all the time. During the summer when she had been so sick, Mrs. Bailey had arranged for Molly to temporarily ride Jessa's pony. The only thing was, now that Jessa was back on her feet, Molly was still riding Rebel all the time. Not only that, Mrs. Bailey seemed determined to keep Jessa on Jasmine, her own big chestnut mare, even though the horse was proving to be far more difficult to ride than Jessa had hoped. The warmblood was so completely different from Rebel, Jessa felt as if she were learning to ride all over again.

"One more time, Jessa? How about you trot in this time?"

Jessa picked up her reins and moved Jasmine forward. It was plain insulting that she had to trot fences when Molly, who was only eight, was allowed to canter. There was no way Jessa was going to argue with Mrs. Bailey, though. Getting on the wrong side of the feisty old woman would mean the biggest thing Jessa would ride would be her bicycle. She choked back her protest and asked Jasmine to trot.

"There, now, that's a lovely trot, Jessa. Light hands, that's it. Shorten up your reins a little—make sure you get her straight to the first fence—no, no! Where are you going??"

"I was doing the course over again."

"Just do the two fences where you had the trouble. Take a circle at the end of the ring and then come down the line. Approach in the trot and then let her canter through the line in six."

Jessa gritted her teeth and tried again. Jasmine swished her tail.

"Be patient! Wait for the jump, stay back in the tack . . . good! Better! Keep your leg on."

With the slow approach, Jasmine didn't have much momentum, and after two canter strides she fell back into a trot.

"That's all right—trot the second one, too."

Jasmine half trotted, half jumped the vertical and shook her head on the other side. Jessa slumped back into the saddle. It was hopeless.

"Jessa! Finish up properly. Show me a nice circle—such sloppy riding! Pretend you are in a show. Make sure you are always working up there. Ride every step of the way."

A show? Not likely. Jessa could not imagine ever going to another horse show—not riding like that!

Mrs. Bailey sighed and spat in the dirt, a gesture she usually reserved for moments when she felt particularly disgusted. "That's enough for today. Now give Jasmine a loose rein and cool her out. Molly? Would you like to go one more time?"

Molly nodded but Jessa didn't stop to watch. She carefully kept her back to the younger girl and her obnoxiously bouncy ponytail as Molly and Rebel negotiated the little course with what sounded like an absolutely even and steady rhythm.

"Lovely!" Mrs. Bailey clapped her hands. "That was a much better release that time—you gave him lots of room to use his head and neck. Good work! Both of you. And Jessa—there's no need for such a long face. You can only do better next time. You are doing just fine, you know."

"Hmmm," Jessa said. She might be doing just fine if she were a blind baboon. But maybe that was insulting to baboons.

"You coming on a trail ride, Jessa?"

Cheryl sat astride Billy Jack just outside the ring.

"Would that be okay with you, Mrs. Bailey?"

"Certainly. As long as you stay at a walk. Would you like to go along, too, Molly?"

Molly looked uncertainly at Jessa, her round cheeks rosy beneath her freckles.

Jessa glanced at Mrs. Bailey, who was looking at her expectantly.

"Fine."

"Jessa, do you have juice or whatever you need?"

Jessa nodded and patted the fanny pack she wore around her waist. She knew better than to go anywhere without juice, cookies, and glucose tablets, just in case she had an insulin reaction and went low.

"Allow me," Cheryl said. "I've been practising." Without dismounting, she leaned down from the saddle and undid the gate latch. Then, steering with one hand, she opened the gate to the riding ring and let the other two horses out.

"Pretty good, huh? That's what the cowboys did in the Old West."

"If you lived on a ranch today you'd still have to manage gates," Mrs. Bailey added. "Have a good ride, girls. Jessa, you're not forgetting you have to do evening feed tonight?"

"I know. We won't be long." Mrs. Bailey needn't have worried. Jessa couldn't imagine a fate worse than spending time with Molly, especially when it meant Jessa had to watch Molly ride Rebel.

"Where do you want to go?" Cheryl asked. "To the beach?"

Jessa shook her head. "Not that far. How about as far as the railway shack?"

Cheryl gave her a strange look. "But that will only take ten minutes."

"That's okay," Molly said quickly. "My mom's coming to pick me up pretty soon anyway."

For just a moment Jessa felt triumphant and then, just as quickly, she felt awful. She really liked going on trail rides. It took hardly any time at all to get to the shack and then they'd be done. She sighed. Why was everything going wrong? With Molly tagging along, she couldn't even talk to Cheryl about all the stuff that was bothering her.

"Fine," she said aloud. "To the railway shack and back."

"Fine," Cheryl said, though she didn't sound very fine.

Great. Now she was making everyone else miserable, too. Jessa wished she could go home and start the whole day over again.

3

"This is one of the major projects for the year. Please make sure it is handed in on time—ten percent will be deducted from your grade for each day your project is late." Mr. Denyer gave a little grunt and puffed out his cheeks. "Now—" His cheeks deflated back to normal size. "Back to the Nile River. Can anyone tell me three reasons that the Nile . . ."

Jessa groaned. How much homework did they expect her to be able to do? Didn't they realize she was at the barn every day after school? Not only had Mr. Denyer assigned a big project about ancient Egypt, Mr. Small expected two book reports each term—and that was in addition to the regular novel studies they would do together as a class.

"Jessa?"

"Excuse me?"

Mr. Denyer grunted again and pinched the tip of his nose between his thumb and forefinger, almost as if he were trying to keep out a bad smell. Jessa might have taken it personally except Mr. Denyer pinched his nose every time someone stopped listening to him—which was often.

"Why was the Nile River so important to the people of ancient Egypt?"

What Jessa wanted to say was *Why should I care?* The dumb Egyptians had been dead for a gazillion years and had lived on the far side of the globe. Jessa couldn't really see the point in studying them at all, but with Mr. Denyer glaring at her, she could hardly speak her mind. The red-haired teacher pinched the tip of his nose again.

"Umm . . . the river was important because . . ."

"Yes?"

A flash of inspiration came to Jessa. Dark Creek ran right through the upper field at the barn.

"So the Egyptian horses had somewhere to drink?"

Mr. Denyer opened his mouth to say something and then stopped after drawing in a sharp breath. "Well, yes, livestock would have to drink, certainly. Does anybody else have any other suggestions?"

Jessa lowered her eyes to stare into her textbook. A photograph of several pyramids stared back at her. Out of the corner of her eye she noticed Andrew Timmins' leg had stopped jiggling. She could feel his eyes on her and she blushed. Jessa turned her shoulders so she was twisted slightly sideways in her desk and didn't have to look at him. A moment later she heard the *tick-tick-tick* of his desk rattling as Andrew's leg began its familiar twitching. She would never get used to that racket. Not ever.

"I don't know why he sits beside me in every class we have together," Jessa complained to Cheryl at lunch. "He can't sit still. He's always wiggling around and jiggling his leg up and down like this."

"Whoa, watch out—your soup!"

Jessa pushed her tray back on the table, well clear of

her leaping knee. "I can't stand him."

"So move."

"Can't. We have assigned seats."

"So ignore him."

"Easy for you to say. You don't have to . . ." Jessa stopped as Andrew passed their table. Don't sit here, keep going, she thought as his gaze rested a moment on the empty chair beside hers. Andrew didn't stop, though. He chose a table over by the window and sat with his back to her and Cheryl.

"That was close," she said. "Even his hair is weird. There's a piece at the back of his head that's always sticking up."

Cheryl tipped her head to one side. "He doesn't look that bad. A bit skinny, maybe, but that's not a crime. He's new. He's probably nervous."

"We're all new here. That's no excuse for behaving like an idiot. I'm new and I don't jerk my legs around so much it drives everyone else in the room crazy."

Cheryl tossed her shock of red curls. "Harsh words, my dear. Harsh words. You have some less than charming qualities, too, you know."

Jessa blew on a spoonful of soup and scowled at her friend. "You don't have to defend him. You don't even know him."

"You don't have to hate him. You don't know him much better than I do. He's in my computers class. Maybe I should ask him if he wants to be in my project group."

"Ow!" Jessa spat her mouthful of soup back into the bowl. It was still too hot to eat. She crumbled a package of crackers into the steaming yellow mixture and stirred.

"Can you eat that?"

"Leave me alone. I'm adding up the exchanges in my head." Jessa knew she needed to eat a certain amount at lunchtime to balance out the amount of insulin she had taken in her shot that morning. It was a nuisance, but she was getting used to figuring out what she needed to eat and when.

"Jessa . . ."

"What?"

"Nothing."

"You were going to say something. Spit it out."

"Nothing. I was just going to say—well, you have been in a bad mood ever since school started."

"No kidding, Sherlock. I don't want to be here. I hate school."

Cheryl pushed her eyebrows together. "Whatever you say, my dear. Who am I to argue?"

An awkward silence settled between the two girls.

"Cheryl?"

"Hmmm?"

"You riding today?"

Cheryl grinned and the tension between them eased. "But of course! Where else would I wish to be on a fine Thursday such as this? And you?"

Jessa nodded, an answering grin tugging at the corners of her mouth. "Molly won't be there today."

"So you're riding Rebel?"

Jessa nodded and her smile broadened.

"Do you have a lesson?"

"Nope."

"So we can go on a trail ride?"

"Yup."

"Excellent. Most excellent! Are you going home first?"

"Yup. I'm going to take Romeo. I'll go home, have a snack, and then ride my bike down. Where do you want to meet me?"

"At your house. We can ride to the barn together."

"Okay. Sounds like a plan."

"Maaahvelous, dahling. Maaaaahvelous."

For the rest of the day Jessa did her best to tune out whatever the teachers had to say. Instead, she imagined herself astride Rebel, trotting along the Dark Creek Railway Trail, the autumn sunshine warm on her back. She could hardly wait.

"Why don't we do the stalls first and feed when we get back?"

Jessa's shoulders drooped. Rebel poked his nose over the paddock fence and she rubbed his face.

"That way we don't have to rush back," Cheryl reasoned. "Come on."

Cheryl turned and marched across the yard to the shavings barn. She loaded the shovel, plastic pitchforks, and straw broom into the big wheelbarrow and trundled her load over to the main barn. Jessa sighed. Her friend was right. It was better to get the chores out of the way before they rode.

"I'll do Billy Jack's stall," Cheryl said. "You can start with Jasmine's."

Jessa flipped on the radio on her way into the big box stall and started heaving the manure and soiled bedding into the wheelbarrow. She quickly settled into the familiar rhythm of scooping and tossing, scooping and tossing. In the next stall over, Cheryl was singing along to the songs on the radio at the top of her voice.

"Whoa, ho, ho baaaaaby . . ."

Jessa slipped out of Jasmine's stall to see if Cheryl was finished with the aluminum shovel. Her friend's back was to the stall door and when Jessa saw what she was doing, she slapped her hand over her mouth to stop herself from laughing.

Cheryl's lips were practically kissing the end of the pitchfork handle. She crooned into her pretend microphone, wiggling her hips and pointing her free hand at an imaginary audience seated over in the water bucket.

"My-ay-ay-ay heart belongs to yoooooouuuuu. . . ."

Cheryl swung around and pointed right at the door.

"Ahhh!" Her pale skin flushed deep red. "How long have you been standing there?"

Jessa whooped. "My-ay-ay heart . . ." Through giggles she mimicked Cheryl's singing.

"That's not bad, Jessa. We should start a band." Cheryl ran her hand through her mess of red curls as if preening before a mirror. "Cheryl and the Dropping Pickers!" She laughed and then attacked a pile of fresh manure in the corner. "Are you nearly done?" she asked.

"More done than you. Some of us are actually cleaning stalls instead of doing the Dark Creek Concert Tour."

Cheryl dipped her fingers in the water bucket and flicked them at Jessa. Still laughing, Jessa ducked back out of the stall with the shovel. She scraped up the wet shavings from the rubber mats in Jasmine's stall and then moved along the row to do Brandy's. She was nearly finished when Cheryl finally started on Babe's stall.

After that, the girls moved over to the little barn and cleaned out the last two stalls belonging to Rebel and the Canadian mare, Sienna.

"Can we go now?"

"Let's put the shavings in, do the water, and then we can go."

Jessa sighed. It almost seemed like Cheryl was deliberately delaying.

"Why don't we finish when we get back?"

"That's why. . . ." Cheryl bobbed her head and looked over Jessa's shoulder. Jessa turned around just as Romeo hopped up from where he had been lying in the sun and bounded over to Mrs. Bailey.

"Hello, girls. How are you doing with the stalls?"

"Nearly done," Jessa said. "We're just going to finish the bedding and the water and then we're going on a trail ride."

"Excellent. I'm sure Rebel will enjoy that. How has Billy Jack been going for you, Cheryl?"

"Great!" Cheryl said and Jessa grinned. Only Cheryl could love a horse like Billy Jack. He was old and slow and pretty ugly, but he and Cheryl got along really well. "I've been massaging his legs after every ride. I think he likes that. Keeps his blood flowing."

Mrs. Bailey squinted down at the girls from under her black cowboy hat. "I daresay it does, yes." She touched her hand to her lower back. "When can you ride Jasmine again, Jessa?"

Jessa coughed. "I guess on Saturday."

"Hmmph."

It was hard to know what Mrs. Bailey meant with her little harrumphing noise.

"Unless you'd rather I rode her on Sunday. . . ."

"Well, in truth I would rather you rode Jasmine on both days. I believe Molly is going to take Rebel in the cross-poles class at Arbutus Lane. They're having a training show at the end of the month so she'll need some extra time to practise between now and then."

Jessa bristled. "What classes can I ride him in?"

Mrs. Bailey pushed the front of her hat up and peered hard at Jessa. Jessa wanted to look away from those bright blue eyes but couldn't.

"Why not ride Jasmine?"

"At the horse show?"

"There's no need to sound so horrified. Jasmine is a wonderful horse—"

29

"I know, I know. It's not that. . . . It's just . . ."

"You can ride her in a flat class, if you would feel more comfortable."

It was uncanny how Mrs. Bailey seemed able to read Jessa's mind. The thought of jumping Jasmine in a riding lesson was bad enough. But at a horse show?

"Would you like to take her in a hack class or two?"

That didn't seem quite so bad, though Jessa knew she would still rather ride Rebel. She knew what to do with Rebel. The two of them would look great together, no matter what classes they entered. "I guess so. . . ."

"Ooooohhhh! That's so exciting!" Cheryl bounced up and down and hugged first Jessa and then Mrs. Bailey. The commotion made Romeo all excited and he barked and raced around in circles.

"Romeo! Calm down!"

"Honestly!" Mrs. Bailey exclaimed, but she laughed and crouched down to call Romeo to her. "Come here, you silly dog. It's just a little horse show. Nothing to get all worked up about."

The older woman might have been talking to the dog, but Jessa knew the words were intended for her ears.

"Well, I'm off to pick up the horse blankets from the tack store. Won't be long before the horses will need them at night. Have a good ride, girls."

4

"We don't have to stop here today," Jessa said as Cheryl halted Billy Jack close to the spot where they had turned around on the ride with Molly.

"I know, I know. When we stopped here the other day I noticed something," Cheryl said. "We can keep going in a minute."

"What are you looking at?"

"Have you ever been down here?" Cheryl pointed at a narrow trail leading off to the right. It was so overgrown Jessa wouldn't even have noticed it if Cheryl hadn't pointed it out.

Jessa shook her head.

"Maybe it goes to the railway shack," Cheryl said.

Jessa shrugged and patted Rebel's neck. "Maybe."

The old railway shack was tucked into the trees beside the Dark Creek Railway Trail. It was hard to see even though it wasn't very far from the main trail. A tangle of brambles and ivy covered most of the small building. Only the peak of the roof and a crooked old chimney stuck up high enough to be seen easily. Jessa had no idea how old the building was or how long it had been there.

"Do you want to ride in and see?"

Jessa looked warily at the thick underbrush. Bushes from both sides of the little path had grown across the trail.

"We'll never get through there. It's too overgrown."

"Billy Jack will push through, won't you, boy?"

Cheryl didn't wait but urged Billy Jack forward. The bushes were chest high and the footing uneven, but he stepped onto the trail and forced his way through. Twigs snapped and Jessa held Rebel back so he didn't get hit in the face by a branch whipping backwards.

Ahead, Cheryl hunched forward over the saddle, one hand up to protect her face, the other holding the reins.

"Come on, Romeo," Jessa called to her dog, who seemed reluctant to get too close.

"I can't see where I'm going!"

"Left! More to the left," Jessa shouted.

Billy Jack crashed through more bushes and Cheryl yelped. "Ow!"

"What happened? Are you okay? Whoa, Rebel."

Rebel's hooves stepped lightly in place but Jessa sat tight and held him firmly. Cheryl and Billy Jack had been swallowed by the thick brush. It didn't sound as if they were getting any closer to the shack. It seemed silly to follow them into the bush without knowing where they were going.

Rebel's ears pricked forward and he quivered, listening to the others thrashing around through the underbrush. Jessa jumped when he let out a piercing whinny. "Shhhh!"

Cheryl's scream set Jessa's heart pounding even harder.

"Cheryl!"

Loud shrieks answered and Jessa shouted back in a panic. "Cheryl! What's going on? Are you okay?"

Jessa's skin crawled when she heard loud crashes and snapping twigs punctuated by Cheryl screaming, "Get away from me!"

"Cheryl!"

Billy Jack and Cheryl burst through the bushes, pushed right past Rebel, and plunged back onto the main trail. Rebel whirled around and followed them, nearly sending Jessa tumbling right over his shoulder. Tears streamed down Cheryl's face and her arms were streaked with bright red scratches.

"What happened?" Jessa asked, alarmed.

"Go! Go on!" Cheryl shouted, waving her arms around. Billy Jack leaped forward and gave a mighty buck and Rebel half reared and pivoted away.

"What!?"

"Wasps!" Cheryl gasped as two wasps swarmed angrily around Jessa. Jessa screamed and Rebel leaped away sideways, nearly unseating her again. Both horses bolted and Jessa grabbed for a handful of mane with one hand and swiped at the wasps with the other.

The girls raced down the trail until finally Billy Jack began to slow and Jessa was able to pull Rebel back to a trot.

"Are you okay?" she managed to gasp. Even before Cheryl could answer, Jessa knew she was not okay at all. Her friend's face was all puffy and red. Her nose ran and her shoulders heaved with sobs.

"They were everywhere," she gasped. "They stung me here and here. . . ."

She held out her hands and arms. They were covered with angry red swellings.

"Ohhhh, it hurts so much," Cheryl cried.

"Come on. We have to go back."

"I know, I know," Cheryl sobbed miserably. "Oh, I can't hold the reins."

Her hands were swelling up. "Look—they got me between the fingers!"

"Oh, that's disgusting." It was just like something from a horror movie. Jessa shuddered and felt like throwing up. She checked her own arms and hands. Amazingly, she had escaped without a single sting.

"They got Billy Jack, too," Cheryl said through her tears.

Jessa turned Rebel around and Billy Jack followed. By the time they reached Dark Creek Stables, Cheryl was crying even harder. "It hurts so much!" she said between sobs. She half fell out of the saddle and Jessa hopped off Rebel and took both horses' reins.

"Quick. Go and call your mom."

Cheryl ran into the tack room to call home.

"There's no answer," she wailed so loudly that Jessa could hear her out in the yard.

"Call my mom," Jessa yelled back. But there was nobody home at Jessa's house, either.

"Should I call 911?" Cheryl asked, staggering back out of the tack room, still crying.

Jessa shrugged helplessly. "I don't know what to do!" She choked back a surge of panic. Couldn't people die from bee stings? What about wasps? "Are you allergic to stings?" she asked.

"I don't know. I don't know." Cheryl's face was bright red and swollen. "I've only been stung once before and not all over like this. Owwww . . ." She rubbed her hands over her thighs. "It's so itchy but it really hurts!"

"You don't look so good," Jessa said, feeling completely useless. "You'd better call 911 just in case."

Cheryl burst into tears all over again. "What if I'm going to die?" she wailed.

"You're not going to die," Jessa said, surprised at how calmly her voice was coming out of her mouth. "I think people who are allergic get reactions right away. But call 911 anyway. Mrs. Bailey's car still isn't here. Who knows when she'll be back."

"But if I'm not allergic and this isn't an emergency can't you go to jail for calling 911?"

Jessa shook her head. "I don't think so. Call them."

She draped Billy Jack's reins over the fence and then manoeuvred Rebel into the cross-ties so she could take off his bridle and tie him safely. The minute her pony was secure she did the same for Billy Jack.

She could hear her friend talking to someone on the phone in the tack room. "I didn't count them—maybe twelve times or something? They were just swarming all over and . . ." Her voice choked with fresh sobs. "Okay. Yes, I'm sitting down. No, I can breathe fine. No, I'm not alone. Okay . . . are you sure? Thank you. Goodbye."

Cheryl emerged from the tack room shaking her hands in front of her.

"They're sending an ambu—ohhh, I can't stand the itching and it hurts so much to rub them," Cheryl moaned. Then, abruptly, she turned and walked away.

"What are you doing?" Jessa asked in horror as her friend marched across the yard to the water trough.

"I can't stand this another second!" Cheryl tore off her helmet and plunged her face and arms into the icy cold water. She was up a second later, gasping, sputtering, and crying.

Jessa ran to her friend's side and put her arm around her shoulders. "It's okay, Cheryl. Everything will be okay. Listen."

In the distance, an ambulance siren wailed. "Owwww," Cheryl howled. Romeo sat with his head on Cheryl's knee, and Cheryl stroked him behind the ears. "Good boy," she said with a wet sniffle.

35

Jessa nodded and patted Cheryl's back. Romeo was such a great dog. Jessa took a deep breath and reminded herself how important it was to stay calm in a crisis.

Crisis. Wow. Jessa hadn't expected to be caught in the middle of a crisis. Not on a gentle trail ride with Rebel.

The ambulance pulled into the driveway and drove up to the barn. Two attendants jumped out and came over to Cheryl. They leaned over her and examined her face and arms.

A moment later, Mrs. Bailey's old Buick rumbled up the driveway. She leaped out of her car and sprinted towards the little group huddled around Cheryl. "What is going on here!" she demanded.

When Jessa saw Mrs. Bailey, she sank down onto an upturned bucket and buried her face in her hands. Now that help had arrived, she felt shaky and light-headed.

"What happened? Cheryl, did you fall off?"

Cheryl shook her head. "Wasps," she said.

"You'd better come with us," one of the attendants said. "Just in case. They can give you some antihistamines at the hospital and keep an eye on you for a bit—just to make sure you don't have a serious reaction. I'm sure you'll be fine."

"Can you take care of Billy Jack?" Cheryl asked through her tears as the attendants helped her into the back of the ambulance.

Jessa looked up and nodded. "I'll keep calling your mom to let her know what happened."

"Thanks," Cheryl said. Then the back doors of the ambulance shut and her friend disappeared down the bumpy driveway.

"Well," said Mrs. Bailey. "I'll give you a hand with the horses."

They were quiet for a while as they worked to take off

the saddles, brush Rebel and Billy Jack, then put the horses in for their dinner.

"Well, I must say I haven't felt so sick to my stomach in quite some time," Mrs. Bailey said. "That is one sight I never want to see again—an ambulance waiting for me at the barn."

Jessa looked up at Mrs. Bailey. The old woman was white as chalk under her cowboy hat.

"Should I walk up to the house with you?" Jessa asked.

"Thank you, Jessa. Yes, that would be very kind. You can use the house phone to call Cheryl's parents again. Hopefully someone will be home by now."

5

"How is Cheryl?" Mrs. Bailey took off her hat and wiped her forehead with the back of her hand. Jessa stopped shovelling wood chips into the wheelbarrow.

"I haven't seen her since the wasp attack—she didn't come to school yesterday. I talked to her on the phone last night—she said the antihistamines are making her sleepy all the time but if she doesn't take them the itching drives her crazy."

Mrs. Bailey nodded and put her hat back on. "Has she tried aloe vera?"

"What's that?"

"Do you remember that prickly-looking plant on my kitchen windowsill?"

Jessa shook her head. One plant looked pretty much like another to her. Mrs. Bailey sniffed. "Before you leave I'll break off a bit. Tell Cheryl to rub it on the stings. It's remarkable stuff."

It sounded rather suspicious to Jessa, rubbing bits of a houseplant on a sting, but she kept her thoughts to herself and said, "Thanks. I'll take it to her later today. I was going to go to her house anyway."

Mrs. Bailey smiled. "I thought you might. Now, let's get a move on, shall we? Molly will be here soon."

Jessa jabbed the shovel into the pile of shavings and made an angry little noise at the back of her throat. Mrs. Bailey didn't hear it, but Romeo, who was lying close by, did. He lifted his head from his paws and tilted it to one side. Guiltily, Jessa turned her thoughts away from all the ways she could make Molly miserable and forced herself to concentrate on getting the fresh bedding into the stalls as quickly and professionally as possible. Dark Creek Stables wasn't a big fancy place, but Mrs. Bailey ran it as if it were a world-class operation.

"Don't bother trying to cut corners," she often said, her sharp blue eyes quick to catch a half-full water bucket or a corner of the tack room left unswept.

Jessa finished scrubbing out the water tubs in the paddocks and jogged to the tack room to collect Jasmine's saddle, bridle, and grooming caddy. The other horses at Dark Creek had the usual assortment of heavy plastic grooming caddies, but Jasmine had a fancy wooden one with her name painted in elegant gold lettering on the side. Her brushes, bandages, hoof pick, ointments, sweat scraper, special shampoo, and mane and tail detangler were always neatly organized. In a removable tray that sat in the top of the caddy, Mrs. Bailey stored braiding elastics, precut lengths of wool for horse shows, and an endless supply of Fisherman's Friend cough candies.

Every time Jessa saw the candies, she had to think of the time she had made the mistake of popping one of the little black pellets into her own mouth. Her eyes immediately begun to water as the innocent-looking candy seemed to come alive on her tongue. It burned and she gagged and spit it out, sending it flying across the grooming area. Jasmine, standing patiently in the cross-ties, had looked at her reproachfully with her large, brown eyes as if to say *What a waste!*

After that, Jessa made sure the horse got one or two each time she rode, but she was never again tempted to take one for herself.

Molly arrived just as Jessa was bringing her things out from the tack room. Jessa put Jasmine's saddle on the rack and glared at the younger girl as she hopped out of the car holding her tall black rubber riding boots in her hand. Molly didn't say anything, but when she brought out Rebel's tack, she didn't take her place at the second cross-ties.

"I'm going to get Rebel ready in his paddock," she said as she disappeared around the end of the barn, her ponytail dancing from side to side. "He likes it back there."

Yeah, right, Jessa thought, and stomped off in the opposite direction, to the big field where Jasmine and Billy Jack were turned out together to enjoy a bit of grass. The two horses raised their heads and watched her and Romeo as they crossed the field.

"Easy, girl," she said, slipping the mare's fine leather halter up over her ears. Jasmine's chestnut coat shone and she eagerly lipped the little piece of carrot from Jessa's palm. "Come on, let's go have a riding lesson," Jessa said without much enthusiasm.

The picture of calm and tranquility, the big mare followed Jessa quietly back across the field.

It seemed to take forever to get ready. There was far more dust in Jasmine's coat than Jessa had expected. "You've been rolling, haven't you?" Jessa knew better than to show up for her lesson with Jasmine in anything less than immaculate condition. She brushed the horse over and over again, flicking the stiff dandy brush to get rid of the dirt. Then she followed up with Jasmine's medium brush and finally went over her again with the softest brush in the grooming caddy. Jessa paid particular attention to Jasmine's head and stood on an overturned bucket so she could reach the bridle path. Even a little bit of dried mud under the bridle could rub and cause a sore.

Throughout the whole procedure, Jasmine stood sleepily, her head bobbing, her tail occasionally whisking away an annoying fly. Jessa was still wrapping Jasmine's front legs when Molly rode past on Rebel. Jessa bit the inside of her cheek and rushed to get the wraps done. In her haste to catch up, she fumbled the black polo she had partly wrapped around Jasmine's right foreleg. The training bandage unravelled, rolling across the ground.

"Oh, no," Jessa muttered, quickly retrieving the unruly wrap. She brushed off the dirt, rerolled the bandage, and started again. By this time, Mrs. Bailey was strolling towards the riding ring.

"You coming, Jessa?" she called.

"I just have to saddle up," Jessa answered, reaching for the saddle. Just as she was about to lower the saddle onto the mare's back, Jasmine took two steps sideways.

"Stand still!"

At last, saddle in place and bridle on, Jessa put on her riding helmet and led Jasmine into the ring. Molly was already warmed up and doing flat exercises on a circle at the far end of the ring. Molly and Rebel looked so small. But maybe that was just because Jasmine was so huge. Jessa checked Jasmine's girth, climbed up onto the mounting block, and gently settled herself onto the mare's back.

"About time," Mrs. Bailey said. "I don't have all day, you know."

"Sorry."

"Pick up a nice forward, connected walk, please."

Mrs. Bailey turned back to Molly. "Very, very nice, Molly. He's moving beautifully for you. Are you ready for some trot poles?"

Jessa sat up straight, keeping her eyes ahead.

"Deeper into the corner, Jessa—don't let her bulge in like that. More inside leg—firmly at the girth."

Great. The trouble was starting at the walk!

"Very nice. That's a girl. A nice walk like that is what the judge will be looking for at the end of the month."

Inwardly, Jessa cringed. The last thing she felt like doing was riding Jasmine in front of a judge—especially not at Arbutus Lane.

Mrs. Bailey put both Jessa and Jasmine through their paces. After some basic work at the trot followed by several trot-to-walk and walk-to-trot transitions, Mrs. Bailey asked for more difficult trot work.

"Now ask for a little lengthening of the trot on the long side—legs—legs—good! And bring her back—balance her—get ready for the corner . . . good! And send her forward again on the long side."

The mare's huge thrust pushed Jessa up out of the saddle as she posted the trot, urging the mare on.

"Great! You're starting to get some extension there—did you feel that?"

Panting, Jessa nodded. After ten minutes of strong trot work, both she and Jasmine were hot and sweaty and ready for a break.

"Give her a loose rein and let her stretch her neck," Mrs. Bailey said. "You're such a goooood girl, aren't you, my darling?" From her gushy tone of voice, Jessa knew Mrs. Bailey was talking to her horse.

"How did that feel, Jessa?"

Jessa nodded and looked down at Mrs. Bailey as she rode Jasmine past the older woman. It had felt amazingly good—the best she had ever felt on Jasmine.

"Now, I don't want you to feel bad about this, but I don't want you to jump at all today—in fact, no jumping for the next few rides. I think this flat-work is doing both of you a world of good."

Jessa bit back her disappointment. No jumping? It wasn't fair!

"Stand out of the way and we'll let Molly have a go at this little course."

Mrs. Bailey adjusted the fences and paced out a short cross-pole course for Molly and Rebel. Molly carefully avoided looking at Jessa as she circled at a slow canter before taking the first jump.

It was all Jessa could do not to cry as she watched Rebel neatly take the fence and canter forward in five perfectly paced strides to the next fence. She hated Molly more than anyone she had ever met in her entire life.

The rest of the lesson went smoothly, though Mrs. Bailey made Jessa stop at the same time as Molly, even though she had started late. "Promptness is a virtue," she said as she let herself out of the ring. "Now, why don't you two girls take the horses along the trail a bit to cool them out and give them a change of scenery?"

Not giving Jessa a chance to argue, Mrs. Bailey turned on her heel and headed back up towards the house.

Molly flicked an uneasy glance at Jessa, who said, "Fine. Let's go. But I don't want to be long."

Molly dipped her head as if she had expected exactly that answer, and Rebel fell into step behind Jasmine. Jessa led the way down the trail, her back stiff and her mind seething. If she had the nerve, she would love to take off, pressing Jasmine into a fast gallop. The bigger horse would quickly leave Molly and Rebel in the dust. Then where would the little twerp be?

Jessa imagined Molly lost and crying. Maybe she would even fall off. Jessa sighed and reached forward to pat Jasmine's neck. Much as she despised Molly, she wouldn't do anything that would put Rebel at risk. She knew too well that Rebel would give his all to keep up—he'd be like one of those racehorses who gallop across the finish line with a broken leg.

The thought of Rebel hurt was too awful to even imagine, so Jessa started counting trees. The section of the Dark Creek Railway Trail closest to the barn was like a leafy tunnel. Large trees grew on both sides of the trail and their overhanging branches formed a colourful canopy at this time of year as the leaves began to turn orange, gold, and yellow. Counting the trees made it impossible for Jessa to think of anything else.

The two horses came around a bend in the trail and ahead, Jessa saw another horse coming towards them. She squinted and pushed her glasses up her nose, but she couldn't recognize the other horse. As the pair came closer, Jessa could see the horse was a dark, dapple grey, nearly black on its haunches and legs and lightening to pale grey on its belly.

The horse's rider looked about the same size as Jessa and she wondered who it could be. It wasn't until they drew even that Jessa recognized the face beneath the riding hat.

"Andrew!" she said.

Andrew Timmins didn't say anything. The look on his face changed from one of shock and surprise to one of horror. Without saying a word, he stopped, turned his horse around, and trotted away in the direction he had come from.

"Who was that?" Molly asked.

Jessa was so surprised she forgot for a moment she

wasn't speaking to Molly. "Ah . . . I think it was a new boy at my school. I'm pretty sure that was Andrew."

"He wasn't very friendly," Molly said.

"No," Jessa said slowly. "No, he wasn't." She couldn't understand why he had turned and ridden off so quickly. Maybe she had been mistaken. Maybe it hadn't been Andrew at all—she'd had only a moment to see his face. Maybe the boy was Andrew's brother and didn't like it when people couldn't tell the two of them apart. Or maybe it actually had been Andrew and he had been mad at her for ignoring him at school.

Puzzled, Jessa tried to think what the look of horror had meant on his face. Surely he couldn't already hate her that much. He hardly knew her.

"Do you want to follow him? See where he's going?" Molly asked.

Jessa shook her head. Andrew, or the boy who looked a lot like Andrew, had already disappeared around another bend. "It's getting kind of late. I have to finish the chores at the barn and then I'm going to Cheryl's house. I can't be out for too much longer."

"Okay." If Molly was disappointed, she didn't say anything. The girls rode along the trail for a few minutes more, each lost in her own thoughts. At the big cedar tree leading to the clearing where Jessa knew of a great log for jumping, Jessa halted Jasmine.

"There's a fallen tree down there," she said, pointing at the partially overgrown path. "It's kind of fun to jump. Rebel can do it. We tried it last year."

Uncertainly, Molly looked at Jessa. "Can we go down there?"

"No." Jessa suddenly felt sad beyond words. It had been so much fun riding Rebel. She'd probably never get to jump him over that log again. "No, Mrs. Bailey wouldn't want me to take Jasmine in there. And Rebel probably shouldn't jump any more today."

Molly nodded, though Jessa saw her look back at the path as the girls turned their horses and headed back towards the barn.

6

"I'm supposed to do what?" Cheryl held the piece of aloe vera plant between her thumb and forefinger as if it might bite her.

"Smear it on the stings."

Cheryl looked doubtfully from the aloe to the bumps on her other hand. They were much better than when Jessa had last seen them. Now they looked like big mosquito bites, except extra pink where Cheryl had smeared liberal amounts of calamine lotion.

"That stuff makes you look like you have the plague."

"Thanks."

Cautiously, Cheryl dabbed the cut end of the plant on one of the stings. "Hey. It doesn't hurt or anything."

"Why would it? Mrs. Bailey wouldn't give you something that would hurt."

Cheryl laughed and pressed the aloe on another sting. "You never know with her. Remember when she took that splinter out of your hand with the suture needle from the first-aid kit?"

Jessa remembered all right. It had hurt like crazy, but

Mrs. Bailey had clamped on to her wrist with a grip of steel and had paid no attention at all to Jessa's scream of panic as the wicked-looking curved needle headed for the heel of her hand. A moment later, the needle withdrew but Jessa was still squealing.

"Jessa? Why are you making so much noise?" Mrs. Bailey had asked.

Much to Jessa's embarrassment, Mrs. Bailey had already skillfully extracted the sliver of wood.

"How much more do you have?" Cheryl asked.

Jessa held up the plastic sandwich bag and showed Cheryl three more pieces of freshly cut aloe. "It's a pretty big plant," she said. "It was like she was chopping off the ends of its little arms!"

"Gross!" Cheryl sprawled back across her bed. "Did you have a good ride today?"

"Molly was there."

Cheryl grunted. "She's not so bad, you know. Were you mean to her?"

Jessa flushed. "No. I was not mean to her. I spoke to her on the trail." It was true. After Andrew had left, she had shown the annoying little rat the path to the fallen oak. Not that she had taken her on it, but she had pointed it out. That had certainly been above and beyond the call of duty.

"Guess what?"

"What?" Cheryl answered, narrowing her eyes and moving the aloe to yet another pink-smeared swelling.

"You will never guess in a thousand years who I think I saw riding on the trail today."

"Jeremy?"

Jessa shook her head. She often ran into Jeremy riding his horse, Caspian.

"Rachel? Sarah Blackwater? Bridget? Monika?"

"No, no, no, and no." Jessa folded her arms across her

chest. "I told you you would never be able to guess."

"So, tell me."

"Andrew Timmins." Jessa leaned forward and widened her eyes. "At least he looked like Andrew."

Cheryl shook her head. "Wow. Were his legs wiggling all over the place?"

"Not that I noticed. But I didn't have a chance to say anything because the minute he saw me he took off."

"What? Why would he do that?"

Jessa shrugged. "I have no idea."

"Well," Cheryl said, dropping the used aloe piece onto the cluttered top of her bedside table, "if it was Andrew, you haven't exactly been nice to him since school started, have you?"

"What's that supposed to mean?"

"I've seen the way you look at him—like if he comes near you you'll bite his head off."

Jessa could hardly argue. Cheryl wasn't far off.

"Still," she said, "that was really rude the way he rode off like that."

"He must have had his reasons," Cheryl said.

Jessa shot her a nasty look. "Whose side are you on, anyway?"

"Nobody's side. He's not so bad. Our computer project is going okay. It wouldn't hurt you to be a little more . . . welcoming."

"What am I supposed to say to him?"

"Ask him if that was him on the trail. That wouldn't be so hard, would it?"

Jessa grabbed one of the throw pillows from Cheryl's bed and tossed it at her friend's head. "Sometimes you sound so much like my mom!"

"Why, thank you, Jessa dear. Now how about you help your sick friend tidy up her room?"

"Yeah, right!" Jessa threw another pillow and then another at Cheryl who, just as quickly, threw them back.

Romeo and Ginger, Cheryl's cocker spaniel, leaped up from where they had been snoozing and jumped into the action, barking and snapping as they tried to intercept the wild pillow tosses.

Both girls were soon whooping and laughing and diving under the furniture to avoid being hit. Romeo grabbed a corner tassel on an elaborate gold cushion and ran under Cheryl's desk, the white tip of his tail waving furiously. Not to be outdone, Ginger chased after him, grabbed the opposite tassel, and tugged for all she was worth.

The two dogs growled, shaking their heads like wild animals as they worried their soft, fluffy prey. Ginger's tassel came away in her mouth and she jerked backwards. She sat down most indignantly, the golden cords hanging from her mouth.

"Give that here, you naughty dog!" Cheryl said through gasps of laughter. "Bad, bad dog!" Doubled over, she wasn't exactly striking terror into her dog's heart. Ginger thumped her tail on the floor and tipped her head to the side. Underneath the desk, Romeo merrily pulled all the soft white stuffing out from inside the cushion.

"Romeo!" Jessa wrestled the cushion away from her dog.

Cheryl stuffed the evidence into the bottom of her closet and leaned on the door to close it.

"Are you ever going to excavate that disgusting mess in there?" Jessa asked.

"Not if I can help it," Cheryl said. "But that reminds me. . . . I've been thinking. . . ."

Jessa rolled her eyes and flopped down on the floor beside Romeo. Whenever Cheryl started thinking, it nearly always meant trouble of some sort.

"You know how in social studies we're studying ancient Egypt?"

Jessa nodded. They weren't in the same class, but they were both studying the same thing.

"I think it's so cool how people dig up ancient cities and then, just by putting together bowls and stuff from bits of broken pottery they find, they figure out what people ate and how they lived and things like that."

"Your point would be?"

"Wouldn't it be fun to do that? Dig up old relics and stuff?"

Jessa shrugged. "Sure. I guess so. But we can't exactly jump on a bus and head for the pyramids."

"Like I don't know that. But we could do an archaeological dig at an old historical site around here somewhere."

"Like where? There isn't anything like the pyramids on Vancouver Island."

"Maybe not. But there are old buildings around that nobody has used for years and years."

"Like where?" Jessa couldn't think of any old buildings in Kenwood, and she didn't think the security guards at Fort Victoria would be too impressed if she and Cheryl showed up with shovels and started digging holes around the grounds looking for cracked teacups Victoria's early settlers might have thrown away.

Cheryl scrunched up her face and then, as she always did when she had an idea, she bumped her glasses up her nose. "Like the old railway shack."

"Hah!" Jessa pointed at her friend's red and pink splotches. "You think I'm going to get stung like that just in case someone left a couple of ticket stubs lying around?"

Cheryl looked positively disgusted. "You never know what might be in there. An old telegraph machine—or maybe one of those oil lanterns? Or . . . I don't know. Don't you think we should look?"

"No. Somebody else would have found anything of value."

Cheryl shook her head. "Not necessarily. It was really overgrown back there. I don't think anyone's been in that shed for years and years. I won't rest until I've gone back to see for myself what treasures lie undiscovered—"

"Oh, please. You're talking like the guy who found the *Titanic*."

"Fine. If you don't want to come with me, I'm going in alone."

Jessa sighed. "And if you get stung again?"

"I won't. I know where the nest is. Besides, I'm not taking a horse with me this time."

"You're not? How are you going to get there?"

"Bicycle, of course. How else?"

"What if the shed collapses on you? Or the floor is rotten and you fall through and get trapped? Or what if . . ." Jessa didn't say it aloud, but what she was wondering was what if there really *was* some fascinating old historical object in there that nobody had found? She would hate to miss out on an exciting discovery like that. "For safety reasons, I guess I'd better come with you."

Cheryl's face lit up with a wide grin. "You shall not regret this, oh brave and true companion. Friday. One o'clock. Meet here with your bicycle. Bring a backpack. And some food and water in case we're out there for a while."

"Friday? We're skipping school?"

"Don't be stupid. Friday's a half day, remember?"

"Oh, right." Jessa had forgotten about the teacher development afternoon. The third Friday afternoon of each month was a half day. That was another new thing

52

about middle school.

"I'll send you a list via e-mail of all the equipment you should bring. Ooooh, I'm so excited! I can hardly wait!"

7

Meet me after class.

Andrew's handwriting was as jiggly as his legs. All morning he had been so agitated he'd practically wiggled right out of his chair. By second period, in social studies, his jumping knee was making his desk squeak so loudly that Mr. Denyer's hand had stopped right over the Egyptian history timeline he was drawing on the board.

"Mr. Timmins, would you please sit still?" He hadn't even needed to turn around to know who was making all the racket.

Halfway through French class, as Madame Hoffmeier was saying, "Repetez, s'il vous plaît," it was all Jessa could do not to throw her eraser at Andrew. She was about to glare at him again when, to her surprise, he passed her the note asking her to meet him.

Jessa read it again. Was he crazy? Passing notes in class was a serious crime. She stuffed the note into her pencil case and stared intently at the blackboard. Madame Hoffmeier was busily conjugating the verb *être*. She read the French words out with precision and care, forming each sound as if it were the most beautiful she had ever heard.

"Je suis. Tu es."

Why would Andrew want to meet with her? Jessa had nothing to say to him. Maybe he wanted to apologize for riding off so rudely. Maybe he wanted help with his homework.

Jessa glanced over at Cheryl, who was hunched over her notebook, one arm hooked over the top of the page so Madame Hoffmeier wouldn't see what she was doing. She was drawing Egyptian hieroglyphs across her page. Jessa could just make out a square followed by a thing that looked a bit like an upright meat cleaver, then a bird, and a sleeping lion.

Cheryl seemed oblivious not only to the French lesson going on at the front of the class but also to the way Andrew Timmins was now knocking his pencil against his notebook. *Tap-tap-tap.*

Jessa sighed.

"Repetez," Madame Hoffmeier said and began to say the French words she had written on the board aloud. Dutifully, sounding like their mouths were full of marbles, the class mumbled after her, "Je suis, tu es."

Jessa squirmed in her seat, trying not to let Andrew see how she kept checking the clock. As the minute hand crept towards 11:45 and the end of class, Andrew's furtive glances in her direction became more frequent and made it impossible for her to forget he wanted to talk to her.

When the bell rang, Monika and Sarah, two more kids who rode and who had attended Kenwood Elementary, left the room together, laughing loudly. Cheryl slammed her book shut and bounded over to Jessa.

"I'll meet you at the cafeteria," Jessa said, ignoring

Cheryl's raised eyebrow. Her friend crossed her arms over her chest and didn't move.

"Go," Jessa said. "I have to . . . um, talk to Madame Hoffmeier for a minute. In private."

Cheryl glanced at Andrew, who was putting his books into his backpack very slowly, and then at the teacher, who was vigorously scrubbing all evidence of French verbs off the blackboard.

"Fine. I'll save you a seat."

When Cheryl had left, Jessa turned to Andrew. "Yes?"

Jessa watched with fascination as a deep flush began at the top of Andrew's T-shirt collar and worked its way up his throat, crept into his cheeks, and turned his ears a brilliant shade of crimson.

"Don't say anything," he finally managed to say.

"About what?"

Andrew coughed and his pencil flipped out of his hand and rolled across the floor. Madame Hoffmeier picked up her books and said, "Close the door behind you when you leave. It will lock automatically." She left the room and quietly closed the door. Andrew turned an even deeper shade of red.

"Don't say anything about seeing me on the trail." For the first time he looked directly at Jessa and she tried to read what she saw in his eyes. Fear? Anger? Hurt?

"Please?"

"Why?"

He didn't answer right away. He tried to unzip his pencil case to put away his pencil and Jessa could see how badly his hands were shaking. "Please? Just please don't tell anybody."

"Okay. I guess so."

Andrew nodded, a quick dip of his head that served as both a thank you and an end to the conversation. He gathered up his books and left Jessa standing alone in the middle of the classroom.

"What was that all about? Why did you have to stay behind to talk to Madame Hoffmeier? You can't possibly be behind with your homework yet."

Jessa slid into the empty chair Cheryl had saved for her. She pulled Andrew's note from her pocket and handed it to Cheryl.

"What's this? Who gave this to you?"

"Guess."

"Definitely not Madame Hoffmeier. She would have written it in French."

"It was Andrew."

"Andrew? What did he want?"

Jessa shrugged. "It was really strange. He asked me not to tell anybody about meeting him on the trail."

"So it *was* him."

"I guess so. But why would he care if anyone knew he was on the trail?"

Cheryl's eyebrows jumped. "Maybe he's a horse thief."

"Oh, please. Be serious for once."

"I'm just trying to help. Do you have any better ideas?"

"No."

"Maybe he doesn't want anyone to know he was on the trail with you."

Jessa gave her friend a shove. "Shut up. I shouldn't have told you."

Cheryl slapped her hand over her heart and pretended to swoon. "You don't want to be my friend any more. However shall I survive?"

"Where did he come from, anyway?" Jessa wondered aloud, ignoring her friend's dramatics.

"How should I know? All I know is he wasn't at Kenwood Elementary last year."

"So, he might have come from one of the other elementary schools—like H.P. Jenkins or Mount Avalon."

"Or, he might have come from somewhere else—Alberta or Ontario or Louisiana. Or Egypt. Hey—did you know I can almost write my name using hieroglyphs?"

"Is that what you were doing in French?"

"*Très* observant. As a matter of fact, yes. Mrs. Wong was telling us about the Rosetta Stone and how they discovered what the Egyptian symbols meant because very conveniently the same thing was written in three languages. They compared the words they knew in Greek to the symbols they didn't know in Egyptian and figured out the whole language from there."

Cheryl's social studies class sounded way more interesting than Jessa's. Who could possibly find a timeline interesting? Mr. Denyer, apparently.

"What are you doing for the rest of the lunch hour?" Cheryl asked.

"Oh—thanks for reminding me. I'm going to decorate the inside of my locker. I brought all these pictures of horses I've cut out from magazines. Want to help?"

"Sure." Cheryl pushed her eyebrows together. "I should do that, too."

"Okay—I probably have enough pictures for both of us."

"No. Not horses. What does a locker remind you of?"

"A small closet?"

"You have no imagination. Think about Egypt."

"An Egyptian closet?"

"Oh, you are so useless. No, a locker would be a perfect case for a skinny mummy. A sarcophagus."

"Oh, how disgusting. You're going to turn your locker into a coffin?"

"An Egyptian sarcophagus was a beautiful thing. I'm going to get a book out from the library today so I get all the details right."

Jessa shook her head. "You are so weird."

"Why, thank you!"

"So, what do you think?" Jessa asked. The whole inside of her locker door was covered with photos of horse heads of various breeds, a rearing black stallion, a herd of galloping mares and foals plunging through a river, and a very cute photograph of a woman cradling a foal of a miniature horse in her arms.

"Looks great," Cheryl said, but she didn't seem to be looking at the photos.

"What are you staring at?"

"Why are you hiding that stuff at the back of your locker?"

Jessa felt herself blushing. She shuffled loose papers over the small plastic box in the bottom of her locker. "I'm not hiding anything."

"Yes, you are. What's in the box that's so secret?"

"Nothing." Jessa straightened up and started to close her locker door.

"Not so fast. What's in there?"

"Nothing. I said nothing."

"No secrets between best friends."

"So now being best friends means I can't have any privacy?"

"No need to snap at me." Suddenly, Cheryl grinned. "I know. It's my birthday present!"

"Your birthday is months away! Why do you always have to think everything is about you?"

"I do not!"

"Yes, you do."

Cheryl looked wounded but more determined than before. "If it's not my birthday present then why does it matter if I see it?"

"Fine. Look then."

Jessa stepped aside and Cheryl, still pulling on the door, stumbled backwards, bumping into two Grade Nine boys passing by.

"Sorry! Ow! That wasn't very nice."

"Being so nosy isn't very nice."

Jessa's pointed comment didn't slow Cheryl at all. She dove into the bottom of the locker, pulled out the box, and ripped off the lid.

"That's it?" She poked through the contents of the box—spare syringes, a bottle of insulin, alcohol swabs, glucose tablets, and some cellophane packages of peanut butter and crackers.

"Satisfied? Put the lid on and put it back."

"Why are you hiding this stuff?" Cheryl said, sliding the box back into the bottom of the locker. "It's completely and totally boring."

"Shhh," Jessa said, looking up and down the hall. All around, students banged in and out of lockers, joking and laughing. Lunch was nearly over and the hall was getting more and more crowded by the minute.

"It's no big deal you have dia—"

"Shut up!" Jessa said, more loudly than she had intended. Lowering her voice she said, "Nobody else needs to know. It's embarrassing. It looks like I'm a heroin addict or something."

"With a bottle of insulin in your kit?"

"Shhhh. Why do you always have to be so loud?"

"Why do you have that stuff in there, anyway? I didn't think you took an insulin shot at lunch."

"I don't. It's for emergencies—like if there's an earthquake or something and I can't get home in time for dinner and my evening shot."

Cheryl looked a little worried. "Yeah, I guess that would be a problem."

"The school made my mom put an emergency kit together—two, actually. The office has one, too. It's bigger. It has a whole jar of peanut butter, some juice boxes, and a big box of crackers."

"I'm sticking with you if there's an earthquake!" Cheryl joked. "I still don't understand why you're hiding it, though."

Jessa turned to her friend, her voice low and urgent. "No, you don't understand. You don't have diabetes. You aren't some kind of freak who has to stick needles in yourself twice a day and stab your fingers to do blood tests. You know how kids hate needles and blood and sick people. I don't need anyone else to know about my little problem." Infuriated by the hot tears threatening to spill over her cheeks, Jessa sucked in a shuddery breath.

"Having diabetes isn't a *prob*—"

"I don't want to talk about this any more. Okay?"

Cheryl shook her head and tugged open her own locker door. "Fine. Just fine. I won't say another word."

The bell rang and Jessa jumped. She pulled her math book from her locker and stuffed it into her backpack. When she turned around, Cheryl was already gone. Jessa hurried to math class and slid into her seat. Even though Cheryl sat just two rows over, she didn't look at Jessa once for the entire class.

8

"Thank you," Jessa said the next day at lunch as a young man dished out a glob of sticky mashed potatoes onto her plate. His name tag said *Hi. I'm Tim.*

Tim nodded, already loading up for the next student in line.

Jessa added a carton of milk to her tray and then scanned the cafeteria, looking for Cheryl. Fighting with Cheryl was so annoying. Jessa never felt right when she and Cheryl weren't talking. When she finally spotted her, Jessa froze on the spot, stunned. A tall boy behind her bumped into her back with his tray.

"Hey, watch it," he said.

"Sorry." But Jessa wasn't really paying attention. She stared across the cafeteria at Cheryl, who was sitting beside Andrew. Cheryl nodded as Andrew explained something, waving one hand back and forth over his plate.

Move, Jessa told herself. She couldn't stand there in the middle of the cafeteria all day.

She spotted Rachel, Monika, and Sarah sitting together at a table with a couple of empty chairs and moved towards them. "Anyone sitting here?"

Rachel shrugged. "Well, well, well—so you've decided to speak to us? We thought we'd done something wrong."

Jessa shook her head, still baffled over why Cheryl was talking to Andrew. "I've been busy, that's all." Rachel and her horsey friends could usually be found sitting together at lunch.

"Pretty weird that we're only in English and computers together," Rachel said to Jessa.

"Yeah. It's different here. A lot different." It was true they were in a couple of classes together, but the way Mr. Small lorded over his English classroom it was pretty well impossible to chat. Mr. Small didn't appreciate it at all if people disrupted class. He'd already sent two people to the office for talking out of turn. No doubt about it, middle school was unpleasantly different.

"So, Cheryl would rather sit with her new boyfriend than with you?" Rachel asked.

"No. He's not her boyfriend."

"He's not? He didn't go to Kenwood. I think he's in my metalwork class."

"Metalwork? Why would you want to take metalwork?"

"Why not? I want to learn to make jewellery and stuff. Anyway, what's his name? Tim?"

"No, that's the food guy's name. That's Andrew Timmins. He's in practically all my classes. I figured you would know him."

"Why?"

"You've never seen him around before?"

Rachel pushed a strand of long, dark hair behind her ear. "I don't think so. Not outside of school, anyway. He seems pretty quiet."

Jessa hesitated before saying anything else. Andrew

had asked her not to say anything about his riding. But what harm could it possibly do to tell Rachel and the other kids who rode at Arbutus Lane? They would surely run into him sooner or later. He would never know she had been the one to tell them. She ignored the nudge of uneasiness in the pit of her stomach and said, "He rides."

All three girls swivelled in their seats to stare at him.

"Don't stare!" Jessa said, and all three turned back.

"Really?"

"Where?"

"What kind of horse does he ride?"

"Does he jump?"

Jessa put up her hands. "Wait, wait, wait. I don't know any details. All I know is I saw him on the Dark Creek Trail. He was . . . he was moving pretty fast and I was heading back so we didn't have time to talk."

"Seriously?" Rachel asked. "What was his horse like?"

"Really nice," Jessa said. "Dark dapple grey—nearly black on the belly and legs—lighter over the neck. It was maybe an Anglo-Arab or something."

The other girls nodded appreciatively. "Sounds like a nice horse," Monika said. "I wonder where he keeps it?"

"Do you think he'll be at the Arbutus Lane show?" Sarah asked.

Jessa shrugged. "I told you—I really don't know anything else."

"We could find out," Rachel said, and suddenly Jessa's skin began to crawl. "We could just ask him."

"No!" Jessa said.

"Why not? He won't bite."

"Because . . . because . . ."

"Ooooh," Rachel said. "Richardson's jealous. She wants to keep him all to herself."

The other girls giggled.

"Guess what, Jessa. It's too late for that. I think Cheryl has already stolen him away from you."

Jessa busied herself with her mashed potatoes. She racked her brain to think of a way to change the subject. What had she done now?

"They're getting up," Monika whispered loudly enough that half the cafeteria must have heard. Jessa's cheeks burned. She wished she could back up in time so she could walk into the cafeteria all over again. She'd sit somewhere else where she wouldn't have to talk to Rachel and the others. And she wouldn't sit anywhere she might be able to see Cheryl and Andrew.

Though she didn't want to look, Jessa couldn't resist. She looked up in time to see Cheryl and Andrew crossing the dining area. They put their trays on the conveyor belt leading into the kitchen and left the cafeteria.

Jessa plunged her fork into her mashed potatoes. Why had she opened her big mouth?

"So, is anybody going to the horse show?" she asked and was most relieved when the girls jumped in to talk about which classes they'd be taking their horses in.

"What about you? You still riding that pony?"

Jessa shook her head and took a swig of milk. "Mrs. Bailey wants me to ride Jasmine," she replied, then quickly added, "Just on the flat for now."

Rachel let out a low whistle. "I love that horse. She is sooooo gorgeous."

"Yeah, she is pretty nice," Jessa had to agree. She didn't need to say anything about how much trouble she was having riding the big mare. "We're slowly working up to jumping."

The others agreed that rushing would be a mistake. "I guess you're glad not to be riding that little pony any more," Rachel said.

Jessa was glad her mouth was full of chocolate-chip cookie so she didn't have time to answer before Monika jumped in with a story about how she had fallen off Silver Dancer during a jumping lesson. "It was a big oxer and we just weren't ready—our timing was way off."

"Your timing is always off because you come at the jumps at six hundred kilometres an hour," Rachel said.

All the girls, even Monika, laughed at that. "Hey, I am getting way better. I'm really trying to slow down but Silver Dancer is just such a little speed demon!"

"I've got to go," Jessa said. "I have to go to the library before the bell. The old Egypt project calls."

"See you later in computers," Rachel said as Jessa gathered up her things and left the others chatting about their horses.

"So, what did Andrew have to say to you?" Jessa tried not to sound too interested.

"How many scoops of pellets for Jasmine?"

"One. And a handful of sweet feed."

Cheryl scooped the feed into a bucket and swished her fingers through to mix everything up.

"Well?"

"You know, I shouldn't say anything because I don't think you deserve to know."

"Know what? And how come you deserve to know and I don't?"

Cheryl reached into the feed bin for half a scoop of pellets for Rebel. Jessa watched her friend closely. She had been allowed to do the feeding for only a little while, and Jessa wanted to make sure she didn't accidentally give any of the horses too much or too little.

"Andrew is a really nice boy—not that you have taken

the time to find that out for yourself."

"So why was he so rude when I saw him on the trail?"

"Rebel doesn't get any sweet feed, does he?"

Jessa shook her head. "I still say he's rude."

"Maybe he had his reasons."

"What reasons could he possibly have for riding away like that? What's with all the secrecy about him riding?"

Cheryl ruffled her short, wild red hair as if she might tame it into some manageable shape, and studied Jessa.

"What? Why won't you tell me what he said?"

Cheryl sighed. "Because he made me promise not to."

"But *I* told *you* what he said to me—about not telling anyone about the riding."

"Maybe you shouldn't have done that, Jessa."

"What! But we're best friends. We tell each other everything."

Cheryl turned away and dug the scoop down into the pellets again for Billy Jack's helping. When she had poured the pellets into another bucket she said, "Sometimes I think it's really important to respect someone when they ask you to keep a secret."

Jessa shook her head, completely baffled. "But what harm could it do to talk about Andrew riding?"

Cheryl pursed her lips. "I can't tell you any details, but I will tell you this. If you knew why Andrew didn't want you to say anything—and it's not up to me to tell you why—then you would understand why you shouldn't tell anyone he likes to ride."

Jessa again felt the horrible uneasy feeling swirling slowly in the pit of her stomach. How much had she said to Rachel and the others in the cafeteria? She had certainly mentioned that Andrew rode—though she couldn't have given away any details because she didn't know any herself.

"You're just saying this to make me feel bad about not being more friendly to Andrew. Right?"

Cheryl shook her head. "I'm saying it because after I talked to Andrew I learned why he was so worried about anyone knowing he rides. And, I have to say, I can't blame him for wanting to keep his riding a secret."

"What did he say to you?" Jessa felt tears pricking at her eyes. It wasn't fair that Cheryl knew all about Andrew's secret, whatever it was. And Jessa simply could not believe there could be any compelling reason Andrew would want to hide the fact he rode.

"Is he doing something illegal? Did he steal that horse?"

"Don't be stupid," Cheryl said with a little sniff. "I promised Andrew I wouldn't say anything and I won't. Sorry." Cheryl looked at Jessa and asked, "Why do you hate him so much, anyway?"

Jessa couldn't meet her friend's intense stare. She didn't really have a good reason. "Sometimes you can just tell that a person is a jerk," she said finally. "All that twitching and jiggling . . . and lying to people . . . to me, that says he has big problems and I don't want anything to do with him."

A deep furrow appeared across Cheryl's brow. "I think you hate him because you hate everything right now—school, your diabetes, everything. If you weren't my best friend, I wouldn't think you were a very nice person."

Jessa's throat tightened. Cheryl, for once, was deadly serious.

"How can you say that!"

"I can say it because it's true. And friends should never lie to each other."

Jessa stood open-mouthed as she watched Cheryl pick up the feed buckets and step out of the tack room. When

68

the horses heard the door open, they greeted her with a chorus of nickers and low whinnies. Jessa picked up the last two buckets and headed for the small barn to feed Rebel and Sienna. How could Cheryl say those things to her? Andrew was an annoying jerk. But thinking of Andrew, she felt horribly guilty about her lunchtime conversation. Things were so bad already between her and Cheryl, there was no way she was going to admit what she had done.

Besides, she tried to reassure herself, Rachel and the other riding girls were totally involved with their own lives, riding lessons, and horses. Surely they would just forget about what she had said.

The two girls continued with the chores, deliberately avoiding each other. Tears filled Jessa's eyes. Dumb Cheryl. Maybe she hated her, too. This thought was too much to bear. She slumped down on a hay bale and buried her face in her hands.

"Hey."

Jessa felt the bale shift as Cheryl sat beside her.

"Do you still want me to come to the shack on Friday?" Jessa mumbled through her hands.

"But of course. Just because you are a bit grouchy doesn't mean you can't be useful."

Jessa managed a tiny smile in spite of herself. Cheryl punched her gently in the shoulder.

"You still haven't sent me the equipment list," Jessa said.

"Tonight. Tonight after dinner I shall send you a precise list of all the equipment you will require to be successful on your first archaeological dig."

"Hey, it's your first dig, too."

"Not exactly. Mom made me clean out my closet on Sunday even though my arms were still itchy!"

Jessa wrinkled up her nose. "Find anything interesting in there?"

"An old Thermos from last year filled with beef stew," Cheryl said. "That was sooooo revolting I nearly threw up."

"You had to clean it up?"

"You think my mother was going to do it for me?"

"Good point." Cheryl's mother was the picture of elegance at all times. She and Cheryl's dad ran a theatre company, and Mrs. Waters always looked as if she was ready to be interviewed on national TV or step gracefully onto a stage to receive some acting award. She was definitely not the type to scrub out decomposing beef chunks.

"How did you do it?"

"I put these plastic bread bags over my arms and stood the Thermos on the stump in the backyard. Then I held my breath, twisted off the lid, and stepped back to get the hose. I sort of squirted the worst of the globs out from a distance."

"Oh, yuck."

"The worst part was when Ginger kept trying to get in the way—I thought she was going to lick some up and die of food poisoning!"

The girls laughed and Jessa felt the knot in her stomach loosen. Everything would be okay between her and Cheryl. And tomorrow, she vowed, she would talk to Andrew herself and find out exactly what was going on. If Cheryl could talk to the new boy, then so could she.

9

"What the heck is all this stuff for?" Jessa asked, waving the printout of her e-mail at Cheryl the next morning. "Toothbrush? Why do I need to brush my teeth on an afternoon expedition?"

"It's not for your teeth," Cheryl said as she twirled her lock with an expert flip of her wrist. "Bring an old toothbrush because you're going to use it to gently brush dirt off any precious artifacts we might find."

"And the notebook?"

"To record the exact position of everything we find. You can do that. You're better at drawing."

"How am I supposed to carry a shovel on my bike?"

"Tie it across your basket on the handlebars."

Jessa rummaged around in her locker for the drawstring bag containing her gym clothes. "Fitness. Why do we have to start the year with fitness training?"

Cheryl shrugged. "We could pretend we were taking this special training course to get in shape for our expedition."

Jessa looked at her friend as if she were slightly mad. Did Cheryl ever do anything without turning it into some kind of game or grand production? The strange thing about Cheryl and her crazy ideas was that all her goofiness helped make even ordinary events far more interesting.

"I like Wednesdays," Jessa said with a grin. "Industrial cooking all afternoon. Almost as good as yesterday morning—a double block of art. Not bad, eh?"

Cheryl nodded. "I had art yesterday, too—in the afternoon. You'll never guess what the first project is."

"What?"

"We're making Canopic jars."

"What is a Canopic jar?"

"What does your class talk about in socials?"

"Timelines."

"Boring. Anyway, when the kings and queens died—"

"Pharaohs."

"Pharaohs died—and other people, too, actually—they did all these things to the bodies to preserve them."

"I do know about mummies," Jessa said.

"Obviously not much or you'd know about Canopic jars."

"Get to the point."

"Fine. They would take out all the person's organs—you know, heart, liver—"

"I know what organs are, thank you."

"Anyway, they put each organ in a specially decorated clay pot—at least, we're making ours out of clay. The lungs went into a jar decorated with a kind of a baboon head, the stomach went into a jackal-headed jar. . . ."

"That is disgusting."

"Not as disgusting as what they used to do to dead people's brains."

"Stop!" Jessa held her hand over Cheryl's mouth and her friend danced away, laughing.

"They used to stick a long hooky thing up through the dead guy's nostril—"

"Shut up!"

"And then fish out the brains . . ."

"I'm not listening!"

"Girls!" Ms. Bingham gave the two girls a stern look and pointed down the hall towards the locker room door. "Get changed. I want you in the gym in three minutes."

Still giggling, Jessa and Cheryl sprinted into the locker room to get changed for gym class.

Wednesday morning flew past in a blur of jumping jacks, notes, and new assignments. At the end of each class they had together, Andrew fled as if he were terrified someone might want to corner him. He was nowhere to be seen at lunch and disappeared completely right after school.

By Thursday, Jessa had decided that the less she said about his riding problem, the better, and by lunchtime Friday when school let out for the day, all she could think about was the upcoming archaeological dig at the old railway shack.

Cheryl's enthusiasm for the project was beginning to rub off on Jessa, who had stuffed an old tablecloth, a fresh notebook, pencils and pens, collecting jars, empty plastic yogurt containers, bottled water, soft rags, a flashlight, an old toothbrush, and a snack of peanut butter, crackers, and baby carrots into her old backpack. She tied her mother's shortest shovel to the outside of the pack and hung two trowels and a small, hand-held digging fork from the straps at the back. With her hat and khaki pants with all the pockets, she looked like a real explorer.

Cheryl pedalled her similarly laden bike up to the front of Jessa's house, and the two girls set off with Romeo trotting alongside Jessa's bicycle. At the end of the block they turned down Oak View Road and then crossed the street, hopped off their bikes, and let themselves into the poplar field. A trail led along the edge of the big field all the way to the Dark Creek Railway Trail. Just before the trail was another gate, which they carefully closed behind them before cycling along the trail.

They passed the place where they would normally turn off to follow the path to Dark Creek Stables and kept going until they could just see the vague shape of the top of the railway shack's roof peeking up over tall brambles and thick bushes.

"We should drag our bikes into the bushes a bit," Cheryl said, "so nobody will take them while we're exploring."

It was easier said than done. The bushes were thick and prickly right to the side of the trail. Brambles with sharp thorns left long, red scratches on their arms as they worked.

"Ow!" Jessa said, letting go of a particularly nasty blackberry stalk.

"We should have brought an axe. I had one on the list but I was thinking we might need it to break down the door of the shack, not chop our way through this."

"We can't chop a hole in the door!"

"That's what I figured, too. That's why I left the axe at home in the end."

"Don't we have anything sharp? Like scissors or some-thing?"

"Oh, wait. I have my pocket knife."

Cheryl dug around in her pack, zipping and unzipping every pocket before she finally found the knife. She also pulled out two old towels and some string. She wrapped a towel around her hand and forearm. "Tie some string around that."

Jessa did as she was told and repeated the operation on the other arm. "You look ridiculous! Like a half-baked mummy!"

"Laugh if you like—I'm going in!" Protected from the

sharp thorns, Cheryl cut away at the blackberry canes with her knife until she had forced her way far enough into the bush that there was just enough room for two bicycles. The two girls dragged the bikes off the trail, pushed them into the space Cheryl had cleared, and then draped them with the loose blackberry canes.

"Great camouflage," Cheryl said, jogging backwards along the trail. "You'd never know they were hidden there unless you knew they were hidden there."

Jessa joined her friend. It was true. The bikes were quite well disguised.

"Should we lock them?" Jessa asked.

"There's nothing to chain them to."

"Let's at least chain them together."

"There," Cheryl said once she had snapped the lock in place. "I'm sure we'll hear the cries of pain if someone tries to pull them out."

"Can we get started?" Jessa asked. "Look how long it took just to hide the bikes. We didn't bring a tent. I have to be home by dinner."

"Fine. Help me unwrap my arms." Jessa peeled off the towels. "Grab your pack and let's go."

"Careful!" Jessa ducked as a thin branch whipped back towards her face.

"Sorry!" Cheryl didn't slow down. She hacked and pulled at the thick weeds and brambles that completely obscured whatever trail might once have led to the shack. Jessa followed behind, snapping off twigs and branches and throwing them off to the side.

"At least we know nobody has been here for a while," Jessa said. "Romeo—come here. Stay with us." Romeo's ears and tail dropped and he turned around and looked mournfully at Jessa. She couldn't blame him for not wanting to push through the tangle of brush. His coat was going to be full of burrs by the time they were done. "I'm watching you. Don't try to sneak off."

"Stay to the left here. I don't want to go anywhere near those wasps. Do you think they have wasps in Egypt?"

"How should I know? They don't teach us that stuff at school."

"Not much farther. Pass me your shovel."

Jessa took off her pack and unstrapped the shovel. "Why?"

"I'll show you." Cheryl took the shovel and began to whack at some short prickly bushes. They were soon crushed before her vigorous attack. The corner of the shack was not more than six paces ahead of them but they could still hardly see the decrepit old building.

"Stop!" Cheryl dropped the shovel and put up her hand before dropping to one knee and rummaging about in her pack. She pulled out a notebook and pen.

"What are you doing?"

"Making field notes," Cheryl said. She wrote the date at the top of the page. "What's the temperature, would you say?"

"Temperature? Why do you need to know that?"

"It's important. Field archaeologists keep track of all kinds of information about the excavation site."

Jessa sighed. There was no point in arguing with Cheryl when she got into one of her moods. It was best to cooperate. "About seventeen degrees, I think. Centigrade."

"Raining?"

"Cheryl! Don't be ridiculous! Look up—do you see a single cloud in the sky?"

"Clear. Sunny. Approached Dark Creek railway shack excavation site from the—which way is north?"

Jessa turned around. "That way," she said, pointing in a direction parallel to the main trail.

"So, that would make this corner the northeast . . . no, the northwest corner of the structure."

"Structure? It's a rotten old shed. How do you even know it belongs to the railway company? Maybe it's somebody's house."

Cheryl looked up from her notebook. "Jessa—look at this place. Nobody has been here for a gazillion years."

"This shack hasn't been here for a gazillion years."

"You know what I mean. There's no way anybody lives here."

Jessa didn't point out that her friend hadn't answered her question about the shack even belonging to the railway company at all. The railway hadn't run along the trail for years and years—not since long before Jessa had been born. At some point, the abandoned rail bed had been turned into a kind of endlessly long and skinny park that stretched for a long way through woods and farmland all the way along the Saanich Peninsula.

"Take a look at this."

Cheryl pulled a piece of paper from her bag.

"What's this?" Jessa unfolded several sheets of paper that had all been taped together. It was a photocopy of a map.

"It's a map."

"I can see that. Where did you get this?"

"From the city archives."

"What!"

"I went to do a little research so we didn't excavate somebody's house by accident. That's a map of the routes of the four railway companies that used to take passengers and freight from Victoria up the peninsula to Sidney."

"Why did you mark this with yellow?"

"That's Elk Lake."

Elk Lake wasn't far from Kenwood.

"See that road marked there? That must be where Mountainview Road is today."

"So, if that's Mountainview Road and that's north . . ." Jessa turned the map around. "We must be right about here."

Cheryl pushed her finger about two centimetres along. "Hey! It says there should be a siding here."

"And," Cheryl said triumphantly, "more importantly, there seems to be a building of some sort."

"The shack!" Jessa looked up at the weathered logs of the old building in front of them. "So, this might really have belonged to the Dark Creek Railway Company."

It was strange. Jessa had always called the ramshackle edge of roof still visible from the main trail "the railway shack," but she'd never really thought of it as being a historical building.

Cheryl nodded and folded the map away again. "Seems like too much of a coincidence to me that someone would have built some kind of tool shed here in the middle of nowhere."

Jessa looked around at the thick bushes and nodded. From where they stood they couldn't see the main trail any more. On all sides a thick screen of bushes and trees hid them. Standing beside her friend, Jessa felt a thrill of excitement well up inside her. This was just like a real adventure! Cheryl was right. They were real archaeologists uncovering the past.

"Come on. Let's see if we can get inside."

This time, there was no argument from Jessa.

The girls worked as quickly as they could, clearing a path just wide enough to get around to the other side of the shed.

"There's a window up there."

Jessa craned her head to see where Cheryl was

pointing. The window was small and filthy. Three of the four small square panes of glass were still intact.

"Can you boost me up there?" Cheryl asked.

"It's too high. There must be a door."

Cheryl edged sideways another few centimetres. "There may be a door, but these blackberries are higher than the roof on this side. I can't get any closer."

"We could hack at them with the shovel," Jessa suggested. Now that they were so close she couldn't wait to get inside.

"Look how thick they are! And how many. A shovel isn't really the right tool. Your mom gardens. What does she use to get rid of brambles?"

"She doesn't have brambles like this. This is like a jungle. They're almost like trees. And look at the spikes on them!"

"Your mom must have something. . . ."

Jessa thought of the jumble of tools in the shed behind her mother's small greenhouse. "Well, she has these big long-handled cutting things. She uses them to prune the apple tree branches."

"I say we go—"

A shout, followed by snorts and the thudding sound of trampling hooves, came from the main trail.

"Whoa! Easy, boy," they heard someone say. "Get away from us! Git!"

With a start, Jessa realized Romeo was no longer behind her.

"Romeo!"

Both Cheryl and Jessa pushed back through the rough trail they had made.

"Easy! Who's there?"

"We're coming!" Jessa called out. "It's okay—it's just us." As they emerged from the gap in the bushes, Jessa saw a beautiful dapple grey horse dancing around at the end of his reins. Andrew, dusty and flushed, grimly held on to the other end of the reins in front of his horse, trying to calm his obviously upset mount.

"Take it easy, Lester. Whoa now. It was just a dog."

Romeo slunk behind Jessa's legs. "I'm so sorry . . . we were just . . ." Jessa faltered.

Andrew didn't seem to care. "Your dog came out of the bushes and spooked my horse." He managed to get close enough to Lester that he was able to reach up and stroke the horse's neck. At his familiar touch the horse visibly relaxed, though he kept looking warily at Romeo, his nostrils flaring and his flanks quivering.

Cheryl stepped forward. "Hi, Andrew."

"You said you weren't riding today," he said. He sounded angry.

"We aren't. We came down here on our bikes."

Jessa saw a look pass between Cheryl and Andrew that she didn't understand.

"We were just leaving. We were taking the dog for a run," Cheryl said. "Our bikes are here." She began to pull her bike out, and Lester took another leap sideways.

"Wait," Andrew said. "Can you hold him and let me ride away before you drag those out of the bush?"

"Are you sure you should be riding him?" Jessa asked. The horse looked pretty wound up.

"We'll be fine, thank you. We'll just walk, and if he doesn't relax I'll get off and lead him."

"Do you have far to go?" Jessa was dying to ask him where he kept Lester, what barn he rode at, and why she had never seen him around before.

"No," he said and gathered up his reins. Jessa stood at Lester's head while Cheryl gave Andrew a leg up. Then the boy turned his horse and rode off down the trail, leaving Cheryl, Jessa, and Romeo staring after him.

10

"Oh, Romeo," Jessa said half-heartedly. Whatever she might think of Andrew and his strange behaviour, she would never have spooked his horse intentionally. Romeo's tail waved slowly from side to side.

"You know you were a bad dog, don't you," Cheryl said.

Romeo's tail wagged a touch faster.

"Cheryl, what's going on?"

"What do you mean?"

"You know exactly what I mean. Why did Andrew say that about us not riding?"

Cheryl shrugged. "How should I know? When we were talking earlier he asked if we both rode and I told him we both rode horses at Dark Creek Stables and—"

"Slow down," Jessa interrupted, putting her hands on Cheryl's shoulders.

Cheryl took a deep breath.

"He asked me if we would be riding today and I said 'No.' Which was true."

"But why would he care?"

Cheryl looked away. "How much time do we have before you have to go home?"

"Don't change the subject. I hate it when you do that."

"Okay, okay. Don't yell."

"So?" Jessa looked expectantly at Cheryl.

"He didn't want to run into you," Cheryl said, turning and walking back towards the path they'd cleared through the underbrush.

Jaws clenched, Jessa followed her. "What do you mean, he didn't want to run into me? What did I ever do to him? The little creep. What is his problem, anyway?"

"Maybe," Cheryl said, "he isn't the one with the problem. Andrew knows you don't like him—you've made that pretty obvious. And he . . . well, he probably has a good reason to stay clear of people who don't like him."

Jessa opened her mouth and shut it again with a soft *pop* without saying anything. She had the distinct feeling Cheryl knew more than she was saying. Jessa hadn't been exactly friendly, that was true. But she hadn't done anything really mean to Andrew, either. So what if she'd mentioned his riding to Rachel and the other girls? Nothing had happened. They'd probably forgotten it by now. And anyway, Andrew wouldn't even know about her big mouth. He could hardly be so mad about her blabbing that he wouldn't want to run into her on the trail.

"Are you coming?" Cheryl called back to Jessa. She was already back at the shack end of the cleared path.

"Come on, Romeo," Jessa said and patted her leg. It was a mystery, all right, whatever was going on with Cheryl and Andrew. A very annoying mystery.

When Jessa caught up to Cheryl, Romeo jumped up so his paws rested on Cheryl's chest.

"You silly dog! Stay here with us this time." With a long piece of string from yet another zippered compartment of her backpack, Cheryl slipped a loop at one end through Romeo's collar and then secured the other end to a low tree branch.

"Ready?" Cheryl asked. "If I hold the canes back like this—" Cheryl pinned the prickly end against the shack with two trowels. "—then you can whack them with the sharp part of the shovel." Cheryl was back on her expedition and clearly had no interest in discussing Andrew and his reasons for being so rude.

Jessa sighed and hit the blackberry stalks as hard as she could. They were tough, and it took several chops before they gave way. Cheryl carefully pulled them aside.

When the girls had cleared enough brambles so they could get right up to the door, they dropped their tools and got ready to push. "One, two, three—push!" Jessa and Cheryl threw their shoulders against the old wooden door. The door itself was quite solid, but the wood around the latch was soft and crumbling. The door shifted and then settled back into its frame.

"Almost," Cheryl said, puffing. "One more time."

The girls slammed against the door and shrieked as it gave way. It swung inward on its hinges, sending them both flying into the dim interior of the old wooden building.

"Wow," Cheryl said, catching her breath. She fumbled in her pack and pulled out a flashlight. The narrow white beam swept over the walls of the shack.

"Look at all the spider webs," Jessa said.

"What a mess. Oh, look—good thing we didn't take another step!"

Jessa looked where Cheryl's beam shone on a hole in the floor. The wooden boards had rotted right through.

"No wonder," she said. "Look up there."

Above them, patches of blue were visible through holes in the roof.

"It must rain right in here. Amazing it's still standing at all."

Cheryl put her foot out to the side and tested the floor. The old boards creaked and groaned but held as she moved over to a rickety shelf under a window beside the door.

"Careful," Jessa said. "You can see the boards bending when you stand on them." She felt rooted to the spot, afraid to move in case the floor gave way and she fell through.

"Oh, disgusting," Cheryl said, pointing at the shelf.

"What?"

"Rat droppings."

Jessa shuddered and looked warily towards the hole in the floor. "They probably live under there," she said, pointing.

"Hit them with your shovel if they try to attack," Cheryl said, using her notebook to sweep dust, droppings, and rotten leaves off the shelf.

"Let's go," Jessa said. "There's nothing here."

"Maybe there's a ghost."

Jessa's skin crawled at the thought of it, and she swore she could feel a chill draft caress the back of her neck. "Don't say stuff like that."

"Look!"

Jessa still didn't move. "What is it?"

"Some kind of poster or something."

"Kind of small for a poster," Jessa said, looking at the scrap of yellowed paper nailed to the wall beside the window.

"It's all faded," Cheryl said, shining her light on the paper and leaning closer to inspect it. "Maybe if I use my magnifying glass." She rummaged through her bag and pulled out the glass. Though she leaned over the shelf and stretched up on her tiptoes, she still couldn't get close enough for a really good inspection.

"Don't climb up there!" Jessa said. "It might—"

Her warning was interrupted by the sound of rotting wood giving way. With a great crack, the shelf collapsed under Cheryl's weight and she crashed backwards to the floor. Her flashlight leaped from her hand and rolled away.

"Ow!"

"Oh, no!" Jessa said as she watched the flashlight roll right through the hole in the floorboards. It hit the ground below and went out.

"Rats," Cheryl said. "That's my dad's good flashlight."

"*Rats* is right," Jessa said. "I'm not crawling down there to get it."

"Thanks. Some friend," Cheryl said, handing Jessa the magnifying glass and brushing dirt and leaves off her backside.

"Are you okay?"

"I'll survive. We can't leave that down there. Dad will kill me."

Both girls stared at the jagged edge of the hole. Jessa took a step closer.

"Stop!"

"What? Don't scare me like that."

"The floor is rotten all around the hole. We have to lie down like this."

Ignoring the filth, Cheryl plopped to her stomach. "This is what rescuers do when someone falls through a hole in the ice. They lie down on the frozen river spreading their weight out like this—" She spread her arms and legs out so she sprawled across the floor taking up as much space as humanly possible. "That distributes the weight across the ice so the rescuers don't fall through, too."

She inched her way forward on her stomach towards the hole.

"Be careful."

"It's working, isn't it?"

Cheryl reached the edge of the hole and hung her head into the dark cavity below. "Pass me your flashlight."

Jessa dropped to her knees and rummaged around in her bag for her light. "Here."

Cheryl's hand reached up behind her back. She didn't pull her head out of the hole.

"Can you see anything?" Jessa asked, passing her the light.

"I'm letting my eyes adjust to the dark. Whew! It stinks down here." Cheryl clicked on the light. "There it is."

"Can you reach it?"

Cheryl grunted and squirmed forward another few centimetres.

"There's other stuff down here," she said.

"Like what?"

"Broken bottles. I've almost got—whoa!!"

With a crash, Cheryl slithered headfirst into the hole.

"Cheryl!"

"Ow!"

"Are you okay?"

"Ow, ow, ow!"

The hole was now considerably bigger. From where Jessa stood she could see only darkness.

"Where's the light?"

"I dropped it."

"Can you stand up?"

After much grunting and groaning, Cheryl's shock of red hair emerged from the hole. When she stood upright, her armpits were about level with the floor.

"It can't have gone far," she said. "I should be able to feel it."

She crouched down and disappeared back under the floor. Jessa tried not to think of the rats lurking down in the darkness. A moment later a light clicked on. Light filtered up from between the floorboards and lit up the hole. "This one is yours. It seems to be working fine. I'll just grab the other one." She crouched back down and disappeared from sight.

"Have you got it?"

"It's gone!"

"What do you mean, gone?"

"Gone. It was right over here. . . ."

There was a bump and the sound of wood and debris being moved aside. "A bunch of wood fell down. . . ."

"Maybe you should just leave it, Cheryl. You could just tell your dad what happened. I don't think it's safe down there. What if the whole place collapses?"

"Wow," Cheryl said.

"Did you find it?"

"Wow! This is fantastic!"

"What? What have you got?"

Cheryl's head popped back out of the hole. She was holding something in her hand. "Catch!" She tossed Jessa's flashlight and then ducked back below the floorboards.

"Cheryl?"

Cheryl's head reappeared, this time with her father's flashlight in hand. She was still holding something small in her other hand. She slipped the object into her pocket. Then she handed Jessa the second flashlight, placed her palms flat on the floor, hopped once, twice, three times, and heaved herself up and out of the hole. She crawled back to Jessa and said, "Look at this."

Cheryl put her hand in her pocket and pulled something out. She uncurled her fingers and there, lying in her palm, was an old, brass-coloured pocket watch.

11

"Let me see," Jessa said, taking the watch from her friend. She turned around and went back outside where the light was better, Cheryl right behind her.

"Can you believe it? What are the chances of finding something like this? It's a real treasure! It's probably worth thousands and thousands of dollars!"

"Shh," Jessa said, inspecting the watch. The face was dirty and Jessa rubbed it on her jeans to wipe off the dust. "Look—it has two dials," she said, pointing at a second, smaller dial at the bottom of the face between the V and the VIII. "Roman numerals. How do people read those in a hurry?"

"Those numbers at the bottom aren't Roman. See— sixty," Cheryl read. "I guess that's another hand for the seconds."

"It's amazing the glass isn't broken."

"Crystal."

"What?"

"The glass over the watch face is called a crystal. My grandpa told me."

Jessa turned the watch over in her hand.

"We have to take it home and clean it properly," Cheryl said, taking it from Jessa and running her thumb over the back. "Hey, there's stuff engraved on here!"

"Let me see!"

Jessa peered at the ornate script engraved on the back of the watch.

R.N.M.
~1898~
D.C.R.C.

"R.N.M.? Railway . . . railway . . ."

Cheryl gasped. She handed the watch back to Jessa and pulled the map from her backpack. "Look!" she said, jabbing her finger on the map.

"Wow," Jessa said, her eyes wide. "D.C.R.C." She read the letters slowly, as if they were a magic incantation. "Dark Creek Railway Company."

Cheryl clapped her hands and jumped up. "This is amazing! This is a real, true artifact. 1898? That's ancient!"

Jessa nodded. As she handed the watch back to Cheryl her hand shook. "You take it. I don't want to drop it."

Solemnly, Cheryl wrapped the precious find in a soft rag and tucked it into her pack. "We should close the shack up again and get out of here," she said.

Jessa couldn't have agreed more. Finding the watch was exciting, but it also felt dangerous. She thought of Cheryl's ghost comment and shuddered. What if someone found them at the shack? Were they trespassing? Would they be accused of stealing a rare artifact? Was that a crime? Would they have to give the watch back? But back to whom? It had been lying around for . . . for a long time—maybe more than a hundred years! Distracted, Jessa pushed away Romeo's enthusiastic licking as she untied the dog.

"Was there anything else under the floor?" Jessa asked.

Cheryl shook her head and pulled the door closed. "Nothing interesting. Broken glass. Dirt. Bits of rotting wood."

"I wonder how the watch got under there."

"I don't know. Maybe somebody hid it there? Or maybe it just fell through one of the cracks between the floorboards. You saw how big some of those spaces were."

"But why wouldn't somebody have noticed and crawled under to get it back?"

Cheryl ruffled her fingers through her hair, lifting the wild red mess and letting it fall.

"We should take it to someone who knows about watches," Jessa said.

"Antique watches. I know, what about one of those antique shops down on Fort Street? We can clean it up and take it downtown tomorrow."

The girls had one more look around to make sure they had picked up all their stuff and then quickly left the shack and the clearing.

"What if they ask us where we got it? What if we have to hand it in to the police?" Jessa worried aloud.

"We could just say it belonged to my great-grandfather or something." Cheryl's eyebrows pushed together. "Don't worry about it. By the time we get to the antique shop I'll have a plan."

Jessa glanced over at her friend and smiled. If Cheryl was good at anything, it was coming up with stories. But for now, Jessa couldn't wait to get back home to examine their treasure more closely.

"Jessa! I'm glad you're back."

"Hi, Mom. Can Cheryl stay for dinner?"

Jessa's mother nodded at Cheryl. "Sure. That would be fine—if she helps you get ready."

"Get ready? For what?"

"Mrs. Bailey called. She wants you to go in a horse show tomorrow."

"What! What horse show?" Jessa suddenly felt quite faint. She sat down on a kitchen chair and watched numbly as her mother handed her the cordless phone.

"You'd better call her and get all the details. No doubt you'll have to be at the barn at the crack of dawn."

Mechanically, Jessa dialed Mrs. Bailey's phone number.

"Ah, Jessa—thank you for calling. Did your mother tell you the news?"

"Not exactly. She said something about a horse show. The show at Arbutus Lane isn't for another two weeks, right?"

"Yes, absolutely true. But that's not the horse show I meant. I was at the tack shop and Suzanna told me about a small training show at a little barn near Brentwood Bay. There won't be very many people there and since there's some sort of clinic over at Arbutus Lane, I'm sure most of the riders there won't bother trailering over. I phoned the owner, Megan Wilson, and she said it wouldn't be a problem if we just showed up and registered in the morning. Of course, we'll have to get an early start."

Of course. "But . . . I'm not ready to . . ."

"Jessa, what you lack more than anything is confidence. I know you can ride quite well once you feel comfortable. They have flat classes and also some over fences—nothing big—up to two foot six."

"I'm not jumping," Jessa said quickly.

"No, no—of course not. I wouldn't expect you to."

"Will Molly be there?"

"As a matter of fact, no. Her family is going to

Vancouver. A pity, really. This would have been a wonderful show for her to get her feet wet."

Jessa pulled a face. What a pity.

"I'd like to load by seven tomorrow morning. See you then?"

Jessa moaned. She quickly calculated how many hours she had left to clean her tack, bathe and braid Jasmine, and iron her good riding shirt.

"I guess so." Jessa's mother mouthed *Thank you.* "Thank you," Jessa added. "See you in the morning."

"Well, I would imagine you have a lot to do," Jessa's mother said. Jessa closed her eyes and nodded. How was she going to survive this?

"Can you sleep over?" Jessa asked Cheryl.

Cheryl nodded. "I'll call my mom and double check but it should be fine." Then she added, "Hey, I wonder if I could take Billy Jack in the show?" Without waiting for anyone to answer, Cheryl called Mrs. Bailey back to check. The look on her friend's face was all Jessa needed to see.

Jessa grinned. Having Cheryl and Billy Jack at the show would certainly be more fun than going alone with Mrs. Bailey.

"Can we go up to my room for a little while?" Jessa asked her mother. "And could you please give us a ride down to the barn after we eat? We have to clean tack and braid and stuff."

Mrs. Richardson nodded. "We're just having soup and sandwiches for dinner. You can eat a bit early, if you like. That way you can have more time at the barn."

"Thank you very much, Mrs. R.," Cheryl said with a grin. "We'll do the dishes before we go."

"Cheryl!" Jessa poked her friend in the side.

"Why, thank you very much," Jessa's mother said. "It's

always a pleasure to have you over for dinner."

"So, there goes our expedition to Antique Row tomorrow," Cheryl said once they had closed the door to Jessa's room behind them.

"We'll just have to go another day," Jessa said. "Let me have another look at the watch."

Carefully, Cheryl pulled the soft cloth bundle from her backpack and unwrapped the watch. "I wonder if it works?"

Gingerly, she turned the small knob at the top of the watch. "Look!"

Jessa leaned over to see. The second hand was moving! "That's amazing! See if you can set the time."

Cheryl tried to tug out the stem so she could adjust the hands of the watch. "It seems to be stuck. I don't want to force it. It might break."

"No wonder," Jessa said. "It probably seized up from sitting around all these years."

Cheryl nodded. "Maybe it could be repaired, though. We can check at the antique shop when we take it in."

"I can't wait!" Jessa said. "What if it's worth lots of money?"

"Maybe you could buy Rebel."

Jessa's mouth hung open. "For once in your life you've had a brilliant idea!"

"Why, thank you. Brilliant is my middle name!"

"No, no, no, no," Cheryl mumbled from somewhere under her pillow.

"Come on. Get up." Jessa nudged the protesting lump that was wrapped in a sleeping bag on her floor. The last thing Jessa herself felt like doing was crawling out of her cozy bed at 4:45 a.m. It wasn't even light yet. "We have to go."

"Go without me," Cheryl mumbled.

"Go on, Romeo—lick her to death!"

Romeo was happy to oblige. Tail wagging, he pushed his nose into the sleeping bag and licked and licked until a giggling, grumbling Cheryl emerged.

"Stop! Get lost, you dumb dog!"

"Come on. Breakfast is ready."

With a groan, Cheryl staggered out of her sleeping bag and tugged a sweatshirt on over her T-shirt. "Let's go."

"Do something with your hair before you go downstairs!"

"What's wrong with this?" Cheryl asked, peering into the horse-collar mirror hanging above Jessa's dresser.

"You look like you stuck your finger in an electric socket!"

"Thanks. I'll wet it down and meet you downstairs."

When Cheryl joined Jessa and her mother at the kitchen table a few minutes later, Mrs. Richardson dropped her bagel. "Cheryl! What have you done to your hair?"

"Like it? Jessa, you're going to need to get more hair gel."

"Cheryl! Now you look like an alien!"

"Sorry. I got carried away. You shouldn't leave hair products called 'Hair Sculpting Formula for Artists' where I can reach them."

"No kidding." Jessa reached out and touched the long ridge of spikes that marched from the nape of Cheryl's neck, up the back of her head, all the way over to her forehead. The last, fat spike stuck out like a unicorn's horn. "Good thing your riding helmet will cover this. I don't think the judge would be impressed."

"I was thinking I should redo Billy Jack's mane to match!"

"Cheryl!"

"Kidding. Just kidding."

"Girls, hurry up with your breakfast. You don't want to keep Mrs. Bailey waiting."

"No," said Cheryl. "We most certainly do not."

"There aren't too many people here," Cheryl said as Mrs. Bailey manoeuvred the pickup truck and trailer into a parking spot under a big tree.

"This spot should do. You can tie the horses to the trailer here in the shade between classes. Cheryl, do you have the entry forms?"

Cheryl nodded.

"Good. Be a dear and run them over to the show secretary. I think that's Namrita Long over there sitting at the picnic table under the sun umbrella. Jessa and I will unload the horses."

While Cheryl sprinted off to the registration table, Mrs. Bailey and Jessa let down the ramp at the back of the trailer.

"Jasmine can come out first—there's a good girl."

The big mare backed down the ramp. Jessa caught Jasmine's lead rope and tied her to the side of the trailer.

"Come on, big boy. Let's go."

Billy Jack stood in the trailer munching his hay.

"We don't have all day, dear. Get a move on!"

Mrs. Bailey stepped up into the trailer on the other side of the partition and reached over to give Billy Jack's lead rope an encouraging tug. He just kept munching.

"This horse is so impossibly lazy he'd rather stand in here all day eating!"

"How about some grain?" Jessa suggested.

"Hmph. There's some in the tack compartment. I thought we might need it to load later, not unload!"

The handful of rolled oats was all the encouragement Billy Jack needed. He backed down the ramp and licked every last morsel from Jessa's upturned palm.

"There's a good boy," Mrs. Bailey said, patting his neck. "Now, Jessa—you'd better get Lovely Lady Jasmine all ready to go. You'll have to redo those two braids she rubbed out and give her hock a good scrub where she lay down last night."

Jessa nodded as she took off the padded shipping boots and rubbed the mare's legs. Cheryl, flushed and panting, jogged up to the trailer.

"Hiya, Billy Jack. Ready for some serious ribbonage?"

"Ribbonage? That's not a real word."

"So what. Billy Jack understands, don't you, boy?" Cheryl gave her horse a big kiss on the nose and set to work taking off his boots, blanket, and head-protector.

"Mind you finish up with a soft cloth," Mrs. Bailey said, hovering nervously behind Jessa.

Jessa gritted her teeth. If Mrs. Bailey was going to cluck around like an agitated mother hen all day, she was going to scream.

"They have coffee and doughnuts over at the concession stand," Cheryl said to Mrs. Bailey. Jessa said a silent *Thank you* to her friend.

"Mmmm. Coffee. Yes, I could do with a cup. Can I get you girls doughnuts?"

"I'll have a chocolate dip," Cheryl said.

"A plain cake doughnut, please, if they have them," Jessa added.

"Of course. No sugar doughnuts for you." Mrs. Bailey looked a little guilty. "I'm sorry, Jessa. I didn't think. Are you allowed to have the plain ones?"

Jessa nodded. "I'll eat it a bit later. For my morning snack. That's fine. Really."

Mrs. Bailey nodded brusquely. "Very well—I suppose you girls will manage just fine without me." She marched off towards the concession stand, a second picnic table manned by a teenage girl with her leg in a cast and a woman with thick, round glasses.

"Thanks," Jessa said.

"Not a problem," Cheryl said. "Now let's work fast so we're done by the time she gets back. You know she'll meet a million people she knows and then . . ."

Jessa nodded. She knew exactly what Cheryl was going to say. "Chat, chat, chat!"

"Exactly."

The girls laughed and then turned to their horses. Jessa was soon lost in the happy activity of grooming her mount, whisking the last specks of dirt from Jasmine's coat until the chestnut mare shone in the early morning sunshine.

12

A very small horse show at an unknown barn wasn't exactly the place Jessa had planned to make her triumphant public debut with Jasmine. In her fantasies, when she daydreamed in French class, or lay half asleep in her attic bedroom, she and Jasmine entered the International Ring at Spruce Meadows at a collected canter. There, before a crowd of thousands, they challenged the best horses and riders in the world. Television commentators reported on her every move as she and her magnificent mare were the first riders all day to go clear at the Devil's Dike.

"Working trot, please. Working trot." The judge was shouting at the riders from the ground. He didn't even have a megaphone. There were only five entries in Jessa's first class, a hack class for horse–rider combinations in their first year. There were ribbons to sixth place.

Jessa smiled and lifted her chin. It might not be glamorous, but no matter what happened, she would walk away from the class with a ribbon to add to her collection. And, by the look of the competition, first or second place wasn't out of the question. Another blue ribbon would look great on the wall above her bed.

Jasmine lifted into a trot and Jessa glanced down to check her diagonal. Great. Wrong one. She sat for two beats and began to post again, this time on the correct diagonal.

Don't concentrate on yourself, she thought, aware that Jasmine was running around the ring with her nose in the air. Jessa applied more leg and played a little with her inside rein. Half-halt. Jasmine settled a little. Half-halt.

The mare was just beginning to trot well when the judge asked for a sitting trot. Excited, Jasmine was strong, and Jessa had her hands full trying to keep the mare from bounding forward into a canter.

"Wait. . . . wait. . . ." she murmured softly.

"And now, canter your horses, please. Canter."

Jasmine didn't wait for Jessa's cue. She was raring to go and when she heard the judge's voice say the word *canter,* she started on her own. Jessa glanced over at the judge and groaned. He had seen the error and was marking something down on his clipboard.

"Rats," Jessa said. She sat deep in the saddle and tried to create the lovely rocking canter she knew Jasmine was capable of performing. Jasmine didn't appreciate the half-halt, the firm leg. She gave a playful buck and Jessa growled at her. The judge, of course, was looking right at them when it happened.

The judge asked the riders to trot, then walk, and then change the rein. Now working on the right rein, Jessa's troubles got worse. At the walk, Jasmine spooked sideways in the corner at the far end of the ring. Having decided there was something dreadfully scary at that end, she bulged towards the middle of the ring once the riders had begun to trot. The awkward sideways dance threw off

Jessa's rhythm and they were halfway around the ring again before Jessa realized she was once again on the wrong diagonal. Of course, the command to canter came just as they were approaching the dreadful, dangerous corner, and because Jasmine was bending the wrong way and glaring at the corner, she picked up the wrong lead.

"Jasmine!" Jessa felt her cheeks burning. Mrs. Bailey's cowboy hat shook slowly from side to side as they cantered past, Jessa trying to slow the mare back down, Jasmine cantering away on the wrong lead. Jessa brought her back to the trot and then, halfway along the long side, asked for the canter again. Once again, Jasmine picked up the wrong lead and Jessa nearly began to cry.

She had just tried to get the lead again when the judge asked the riders to trot. A few minutes later all five horses and riders were lined up across the middle of the ring in front of the judge. One at a time the judge asked each to back up.

"Back," Jessa said firmly when it was her turn. Jasmine backed perfectly.

"Very nice. Thank you."

Jessa patted the mare's neck and relaxed her reins just a little. She could not wait to get out of the ring.

A little grey pony called Angel won the class. Her rider couldn't have been more than eight. Second place went to a woman with glasses who was riding a stocky bay gelding called Misery. Jessa wondered what the horse had done to deserve such a terrible name. Third place was taken by a teenage girl on a skittish young mare, and fourth place went to Cheryl on Billy Jack. Jessa clapped for her friend as she rode forward to claim her ribbon.

"Better luck next time," the judge said, smiling up at Jessa as he handed her the fifth-place ribbon. "You have a lovely mare. I'm sure she'll settle down for you."

"Thank you," Jessa said and rode out of the ring as quickly as she could, holding the ugly orange ribbon down by her leg so she didn't have to look at it.

Mrs. Bailey was waiting at the out gate.

"Cheryl had quite a good ride. That old Billy Jack did rather well, I thought."

Jessa blinked and concentrated very hard on patting Jasmine's neck. It would never do to cry in front of Mrs. Bailey.

"Your next class is in about half an hour. Why don't you cool her out for a few minutes—they've opened up the field down there behind the jumping ring. Then bring her back to the trailer and keep her in the shade until you are ready for your next class."

Jessa didn't trust herself to speak. Instead, she nodded and turned her horse around and rode towards the field. Cheryl was passing through the open gate well ahead of her and Jessa nudged Jasmine into a trot to catch up.

Cheryl was beaming. "Fourth! I beat the mighty Jasmine!"

"Thanks for reminding me."

"What happened?"

"What didn't happen? We had a horrible, horrible ride."

Cheryl's eyebrows bobbed up and down. "You didn't fall off, did you?"

"No."

"So, it could have been worse."

"It could always have been worse, I guess."

"And you got a ribbon anyway."

Jessa shrugged. Though it was true, she wasn't that excited about taking a ribbon home. She had not ridden well and she knew it. No ribbon could make her feel better about that.

"Good thing it's a small show," she said.

"Oh!" Cheryl said. "Guess who I saw?"

"Who?"

"Monika."

"Monika Jacobowski? Our Monika from school?"

Cheryl nodded. "She's in the jumping division."

"Why would she bother with a little show like this?"

Cheryl shrugged. "Don't know. But she is here. I saw her heading over to the warm-up area for the jumpers."

"So she didn't watch our class?"

"I don't think so."

"Well, that's a good thing, I guess."

"They didn't exactly get terribly hot in that class, did they?" Cheryl said, patting Billy Jack's neck.

Jessa shook her head. "Not really. I guess it was a good warm-up class for them. We'll do better in the next class."

"You couldn't do worse, could you?"

"Thanks, Cheryl. My goal is just to beat you."

"Good luck!" Cheryl said. "It's not like you have a highly bred, highly trained, super-glorious wonder horse and I have an old plug or anything."

"Shut up, Cheryl."

"Oh, wait a minute. How did you do in the last class? Fifth? What did I win. . . ."

"Cheryl!" Despite herself, Jessa had to laugh at her friend's good-natured ribbing. Still, if she accomplished nothing else, she would beat Cheryl at least once. They had three more classes together before the day was out. Surely she could beat her friend and her ugly old plug.

"Are you going to bed already?" Jessa's mother brushed her daughter's hair away from her cheek, and her forehead creased with concern.

"I'm fine. I'm just going to lie down and read for a little while. After I hang up my ribbons."

Jessa slowly climbed up the steep, narrow stairs to her room under the eaves of the house on Desdemona Street. She loved her room, but on days like today she wished she didn't have to climb quite so many stairs to get there.

What a day. Things had slowly improved after her disastrous start. Unfortunately, Cheryl's luck had kept pace with her own, and Jessa had managed to beat her only once. That had been in a show hack class where Jessa had actually managed to get Jasmine to lengthen her stride while the judge happened to be looking her way. Billy Jack simply didn't do extension of any kind and his hand gallop wasn't any faster than his regular working canter. Cheryl finished dead last in that class and Jessa managed to hang on to third place.

Jessa took little satisfaction in her placing. Though her friend was grinning from ear to ear at the end of every class, even the one where she was beaten so soundly, Jessa felt terrible about her own performance. She had been riding one of the best horses in the whole show and she still hadn't managed to win anything, even against easy competition.

As the day had progressed, she'd caught Mrs. Bailey watching her intently through narrowed eyes and fully expected that the older woman was going to politely tell her she had changed her mind about Jessa riding Jasmine. In fact, Mrs. Bailey had been very quiet all the way back to the barn. Once back at Dark Creek, the three of them had worked efficiently together to get all the chores done and give the horses their evening feed before the girls finally went home, completely exhausted.

To make room for her new ribbons, Jessa took down a picture of wild horses in Turkey she had cut out of a magazine. Her bulletin board was getting crowded. It wouldn't be long before she would need another one. She tried not to be upset that she didn't have another blue ribbon to add to the place of honour above her bed.

Romeo hopped up beside her when she lay down for a minute. She reached over and took a copy of *New Pony Magazine* from her bedside table and flipped it open to the article on taking care of riding boots. She hadn't finished the second paragraph before she felt her eyes closing and she drifted off to sleep.

On Monday morning, Jessa froze dead in her tracks in front of the bulletin board in the entrance hall of the school. Someone had made a huge poster that read

Congrats on the big win, Andrew T.!

Above the hand-lettered words was a big colour photograph of a boy standing at the head of a dark, dapple grey horse.

"Andrew," Jessa whispered.

Other students jostled past her on their way into the building.

"Not a good place to stop, kid," an older boy said, pushing past her.

Jessa stepped up to the bulletin board and read the smaller writing under Andrew's picture.

Kenwood Middle School rider Andrew Timmins wins the Open Jumper Division at the Jade Acres Training Show this weekend.
Way to go, Andrew! And welcome to K.M.S.!

So, he had been at the show, too. Jessa thought it was strange they hadn't seen each other. On the other hand, people had spread their trailers around a big field. It would have been easy enough for him to have stayed off to one side between classes. He had obviously competed in the jumping, and Jessa and Cheryl had felt uneasy about leaving their horses unattended at the trailer to go and watch. Though they had each managed to take in a couple of classes, neither of them had seen Andrew.

Jessa stood in front of the poster a moment longer. What would Andrew think about having his picture stuck up on the wall like that?

In English class, Jessa was surprised when Andrew took an empty desk right at the front of the class instead of sitting in his usual seat beside her. As Mr. Small droned on and on about writing powerful opening sentences, Andrew studiously stared at the board, never once looking behind him.

At least now that the whole school knew about his riding she didn't need to feel guilty any more. A few minutes before the end of class Jessa surreptitiously tidied away her books so she could make a quick escape. She was one of the first students out of the door and stood just outside in the hall waiting for Andrew to appear.

When he did, she was ready. "I just wanted to say congratulations." Jessa felt rather pleased with herself. He might not be a big enough human being to take the first step towards friendship, but she would be.

"Apparently," he replied coldly before stepping around her and disappearing into the throngs of students bashing in and out of lockers.

"Jerk," Jessa muttered. He had a serious problem all right. Jessa decided she had never met anyone so utterly rude and inconsiderate in her whole entire life.

Jessa found herself fuming over his actions for the rest

of the morning. The remaining two classes they had together, social studies and French, were just like English. In each case Andrew moved to a seat as far away as possible from Jessa. When Mr. Denyer asked him why he wanted to change his assigned seat, Andrew replied that he was having trouble seeing the blackboard.

Oh, right, Jessa thought.

When the bell rang for lunch she didn't bother waiting for him. Too bad about her resolve to be a decent human being. If he was going to be that rude to her, she had no time for him. She stormed off to her locker, slammed the door after she'd tossed in her books, and then stomped down the hall to the cafeteria.

What she saw then nearly made her scream. Cheryl and Andrew were in the lineup together. Andrew was talking to Cheryl a mile a minute, waving his free hand around and shaking his head. Cheryl kept nodding very gravely, and when they had loaded their plates with lasagna and salad, they both headed off to a table to sit together.

"Are you in the lineup?" asked a skinny girl behind Jessa.

"No. No, go ahead."

Jessa stepped to the side, her appetite suddenly gone. She glared at the back of Andrew's head and tried to will Cheryl to look at her. But Cheryl was bending forward over her tray as though Andrew were the most interesting conversationalist in the whole world.

So, Jessa. What are you going to do about it? Jessa steeled herself. She was going to march right over to their table, sit down, and demand to know what was going on.

She took a step forward but got no farther because Rachel came up behind her and said, "Hey, Richardson. I hear you were at the horse show at Jade Acres on the weekend. How did you do?"

Jessa blushed. "Fine. I'm still getting used to Jasmine."

"Are you finding her a bit too much horse for you?"

Jessa wondered if Rachel was trying to make her mad. Well, there was one way to put a stop to that. "Yes, actually. She is a lot to handle. But I'm getting better."

Admitting she was having a few problems stopped Rachel right in her tracks. Rachel actually smiled. She bobbed her head and reached for a container of yogurt to put on her lunch tray. "I remember when I first started riding Gazelle—she was so fast and excitable compared to the pony I rode before her, I almost wanted to stop riding."

"Really?"

"Almost. Nothing would stop me from riding. But I thought about it."

Jessa found herself smiling, too. "Me, too." Even though it was Rachel, it was a tremendous relief to talk to someone who might actually understand how hard it was to be riding Jasmine. "Are you sitting with anyone at lunch?"

Rachel shrugged. "Where's carrot-top?"

"Cheryl? She's . . . ummm . . ." Jessa turned to look for her but both Andrew and Cheryl had disappeared. "I don't know where she is."

"Sure. Why not? Did you hear about the great clinic at Arbutus Lane on the weekend? Angela Daveson is so, so cool. Did you know she was on Canada's national eventing team for four years in a row?"

"Really?"

Jessa fell into line behind Rachel and began to load her tray with lunch. Rachel talked continuously as they helped themselves to salad, lasagna, and warm bread rolls. Monika, Sarah, and Bridget joined them at their table a few minutes later, and Jessa found herself swamped by a sea of words about the clinic and the Jade Acres horse show.

She only half listened, distracted by a nagging suspicion that somehow her best friend was betraying her. Jessa vowed she would corner Cheryl and make her explain just exactly what was going on.

"Hey, Richardson." Rachel tipped her head sideways and Jessa turned in time to see Cheryl sprinting across the cafeteria. She skidded to a stop, nearly knocking Jessa off her chair.

"Meet me after art," she whispered into Jessa's ear. "We have to talk."

Before Jessa had a chance to say anything, Cheryl was off again, dodging around a group of ninth grade girls with sports bags slung over their shoulders.

"What was that about?" Rachel asked.

"I have no idea," Jessa said, shrugging as if she didn't really care. But inside, Jessa found she could breathe a little easier. Maybe, finally, Cheryl would tell her what was going on.

13

Cheryl and Andrew walked out of the art room together to find Jessa standing in the hall waiting for them.

"Hi, Cheryl." Jessa waited for Andrew to leave but Cheryl put her arm out to stop him.

"We are going to talk to her now, Andrew," Cheryl said.

Andrew looked down at his hands. Clay had stained the skin around his fingernails reddish brown.

"Let's go out behind the school." Cheryl nudged Andrew with her elbow. "She doesn't bite. Really." Andrew still didn't say anything, and Jessa looked away. "And neither does Andrew! You two are impossible!"

Cheryl might have been trying to be funny, but Jessa had never felt less amused. Andrew was the cause of all this trouble. They'd never be able to get everything settled as long as he was there.

The three of them walked down the hall in total silence. Cheryl was never quiet for that long. It was creepy. The minute they were outside, Jessa burst out, "So—what's the problem?"

She expected Andrew to remain silent, for Cheryl to

have to nudge him again or maybe even to speak for him. But instead, Andrew glared at her as if he might cause her to wither away just by beaming evil thoughts at her. His hands balled into tight fists, and Jessa took a step backwards as he shouted at her.

"You promised you wouldn't say anything!"

Jessa started to ask him who had spilled the beans, but he barrelled right on, each word getting louder than the one before.

"You had no right to put up that poster!"

"Hey! I didn't—"

"Don't bother lying any more! You were at the horse show. You knew I was riding—"

"But I didn't even—"

"And you knew I didn't want anyone else to know about my riding. You should have respected that instead of broadcasting it to the whole entire school!"

The knot in Jessa's stomach tightened. She drew a deep breath to scream back at Andrew that he was being an idiot about the whole thing, that she had never intended any harm by mentioning he was a rider to the other horsey girls, that he should get his facts straight before accusing people of things they hadn't done, but one look at his bright red face, the tears on his cheeks, and she stopped.

"I hate you, Jessa Richardson!" he declared and turned and ran back into the school, leaving Jessa staring openmouthed after him.

Cheryl tore open the door of the school and shouted after Andrew, "Can I tell her why you're so upset?"

Andrew stopped halfway down the hall and turned around. "I don't care what you tell her. It's too late now, isn't it?" Then he turned and walked away.

Cheryl let the heavy door shut and turned back to Jessa. "See what you've done?"

"What! You know I didn't make the poster. I didn't even know he was at the show. I haven't done anything wrong!"

Cheryl sighed. "There's a really good reason Andrew wanted to keep his riding quiet."

Jessa shrugged helplessly. For the life of her she could not imagine why anyone would want to hide such a thing.

"You know what Andrew's favourite animal was when he was a little kid?"

Jessa shook her head, though she thought she might be able to guess.

"He loved horses like you love horses. For as long as he can remember he has wanted to ride at the Olympics—as a show jumper."

"So? What's wrong with that?"

"Nothing. Except, at his old school, Andrew was beaten up all the time because some of the other boys thought show jumping was a sissy sport."

"Beaten up? But why?"

"They said riding was for girls. Or wimps."

"How could anybody . . . a sissy sport? Controlling a massive animal galloping towards a huge fence . . . a sport for wimps? Why didn't he tell them—why didn't he . . ." Jessa swallowed hard.

Cheryl shrugged. "I don't think you can reason with a bully."

Jessa felt the blood drain from her face. "They beat him up for riding?" She kept saying the words but she couldn't really believe it.

"Not just once. And they didn't just push him around a little. One time they actually broke his arm."

Jessa felt as though someone had punched her in the stomach. "Broke his arm? Poor Andrew!"

"No kidding. He isn't a very big guy."

It was true. Andrew was slim and not overly tall. Jessa

could not imagine how awful it must have been for him to have been picked on for the one thing he loved most in the world. Slowly, it dawned on her why Andrew had been so secretive.

"So, he decided he would try to hide his riding from everyone here at K.M.S.?"

Cheryl nodded. "That's why he came to K.M.S. He doesn't even live in the district, but he wanted to get away from those mean kids. He wanted to start again."

Jessa stared at the top of her running shoe.

"I don't know how he thought he would get away with it, but that's what his plan was. He totally loves riding. He won't ever give that up."

"Wow. And he thinks I put up the poster?"

"I told him I didn't think it was you because you didn't even see him at the show. I also . . ."

Cheryl looked at the ground.

"Also what?"

"I was trying to make him feel better—and trying to make him understand that you knew what it was like to want to keep stuff from everyone. . . ."

The knot in Jessa's stomach squeezed even tighter.

"So I told him how you thought everyone would think you were . . . um . . . weird . . . if they knew you were a diabetic and had to take insulin shots all the time."

"You what! You told him about that?"

"I was trying to make him feel better—so he knew he wasn't the only one who—"

"You promised not to tell anyone!" Jessa protested hotly.

"You promised not to tell anyone else about Andrew's riding and the first thing you did was tell me!"

"That's different!"

"Is it?"

Jessa swallowed hard. Maybe it wasn't so different. She felt slightly queasy. Cheryl didn't even know she had told the other girls. "Now what do I do?"

"Call your mom."

"Why? She doesn't need to know about any of this."

Cheryl laughed. "No. She doesn't. But she might like to know why you aren't coming straight home after school."

"I'm not?"

"Not if she says you can come downtown with me. I have the watch in my pocket. Anthony said he would give us a ride downtown to Antique Row."

Still shaken, Jessa looked at Cheryl. "I'll call her. But we have to talk about Andrew. I have to find a way to apologize or something. What if he gets beaten up here and it's all my fault? I'll kill the person who put up that poster!"

"That's a bit harsh. Whoever it was probably wanted to contribute in a positive way to the school community."

Jessa sighed. She couldn't even bring herself to smile at Cheryl's impersonation of their well-meaning principal. Jessa wondered if he'd still be so enthusiastic about the School Spirit board if he knew how much trouble it was causing.

Maybe going downtown with Cheryl was a good idea, a distraction. She decided she could try to figure out how to make things up to Andrew later. "Let me go and phone Mom and get my homework from my locker. I guess I can't do anything more about this mess today."

The man in the Old Tymes, Good Tymes antique shop looked like an antique himself. He wore a fancy embroidered waistcoat with an elegant gold chain looped from the small pocket holding his pocket watch to one of his buttonholes. Wire-rimmed glasses perched at the end of his nose and he peered over the top of these as Cheryl and Jessa walked into the store.

"Good afternoon, ladies. How might I be of service this afternoon?"

Jessa looked at the floor so she didn't start to laugh at being addressed so quaintly.

"We were wondering if you could tell us if this watch is worth anything," Cheryl replied, handing him the pocket watch.

"Ah, a Waltham railway watch," he said, examining it closely. "Let's have a look how old this is."

He turned the watch over and deftly unscrewed the back. Inside, the girls could see the inner workings of the watch. The man read off the serial number engraved inside. "Eight-one-two-three-two-six-two . . . hmmm . . . eight million series . . . that would be . . ."

He pulled out a fat reference book, flipped to the index, and then turned to a list of Waltham serial numbers.

"Here we go. All watches with serial numbers in this range were made in 1897. Lovely watch—not much wear. If you want to sell it, you'll have to get your parents' permission."

"No," Cheryl said. "We don't want to sell it. We were just curious about it."

"Where did you get it?"

"Garage sale. It was in a bag of costume jewellery."

Jessa looked at her friend. Wow. Cheryl really was good at coming up with stories.

The man whistled. "Lucky find. Sometimes things happen that way."

"How do you know it's a railway watch?"

"Few things. First, it says 'railway' in here."

The girls peered at the script engraved inside the back of the watch.

"And railway watches typically don't have covers. That's so the station masters could quickly see what time the train arrived at and then left the station. Did you try to set the time?"

Cheryl nodded. "That part seems to be broken."

The man smiled. "Not at all. These watches couldn't be reset like regular pocket watches. You have to do that inside here. That's so the station masters couldn't change the time to make the trains look like they were running on schedule when they really weren't."

Cheryl's eyes widened. "Really?"

Jessa watched as he screwed the back on again and inspected the engraving on the back.

"D.C.R.C."

"Dark Creek Railway Company," Jessa said.

"That's right. It's a good thing the owner of this watch couldn't adjust the time or he might have been tempted every day. Those trains that ran up the peninsula were always late!"

"How could we find out who owned it?" Cheryl asked.

"Might not be possible. But I would guess that R. N. M. would be the initials of the owner—and 1898 was likely the year he received this watch. In 1898, chances are the owner was a man and probably a railway employee. You know, there are a couple of great local history titles about the railway companies that operated out on the Saanich Peninsula. Why don't you go to the library and see if the reference librarian can point you in the right direction?"

"Okay. We have time for that, don't we, Jessa?"

Jessa nodded. "As long as it doesn't take too long." She looked at Mr. Antique. "So, how much would a watch like this be worth?"

The antique dealer pulled a small object from his pocket. It looked like a little black cup with a piece of glass in it—like a tiny, short telescope. He took off his glasses and fitted the magnifying glass to his eye. He turned the watch this way and that under the light, scrutinizing every worn spot. He unscrewed the back again and peered at the watch workings, wound the watch, and looked at it again.

"Couple of hundred bucks, maybe."

Jessa swallowed. "Really? Is that all?"

"It is in quite good shape, but not an extraordinary specimen." He put the watch on the counter. "But as I said, I can't buy it from you unless your parents—"

"No, no. It's okay. I was just curious."

There was no point in selling the watch. Rebel was worth quite a bit more than two hundred dollars. Besides, if the antique dealer was going to sell it for two hundred, he probably wouldn't pay more than half that to buy it, and Jessa knew that to be fair she would have to split the selling price with Cheryl. The amount left over would be hardly enough to keep Rebel in hay for a month.

She sighed. "Do you want to go to the library?"

Cheryl nodded.

"If you have any more questions, don't hesitate to give me a call," the man said as they walked to the door.

"Thanks very much for all your help," Cheryl said, and the girls left the store together and headed for the library.

"This book should have the information you are looking for," the librarian at the reference desk said, pushing a fat book called *History of Vancouver Island Railway Companies* over the counter.

Cheryl lifted the book and the girls took it to a nearby table and began flipping through it.

"There were a lot of railway companies that went from Victoria to Sidney," Jessa said. "Too bad there aren't any left. It would be fun to take the train, don't you think?"

Cheryl nodded. "Look at this list," she said, pointing at a page at the back of the book. "It shows when each railway was built, lists the dates of major accidents, and then shows when each one went out of business."

"They didn't last too long, did they?"

Cheryl shook her head and turned the page.

"Look!" she said, pointing at another list. "Employees of all the companies. Here's the Victoria and Sidney Railway, the Victoria Terminal Railway and Ferry Company. . . . Here it is—the Dark Creek Railway Company."

She ran her finger down the list. "Robert Nigel McDougall. R. N. M.!"

"Shhhh, don't shout," Jessa said, smiling apologetically at a man at the other end of the table who was scowling in their general direction. "Why is there an asterisk after his name?"

Cheryl pointed at the footnote at the bottom of the page.

d. 1918. See article p. 142.

She flipped through the pages and gasped at the headline.

Dark Creek Railway Employee
Killed in Mountain Lion Attack

Jessa read over Cheryl's shoulder. The details were scanty. Robert Nigel McDougall, an employee of the Dark Creek Railway Company, was attacked while on duty at the Mountainview spur. Despite serious injuries, he managed to crawl back to a railway storage building close by, where he lay bleeding for several hours before being discovered by another railway worker. He died twelve days later of blood poisoning.

A second clipping was an obituary that had run in the local paper after his death. It named several surviving family members: his beloved wife, Emily Anne McDougall, and his three adult children, Ellen, John, and Elizabeth.

"Aww, look. It says here that 'his daughter Elizabeth has decided to go ahead with her wedding to Mr. Albert Woods as she believes it would have been her father's wish that she do so despite this tragic accident.'"

"I wonder if any of these people's descendents still live here?" Jessa wondered aloud.

Cheryl turned to her and leaned close. "Wouldn't it be cool if we could find a relative?"

"Sure. But how?"

"The phone book." It was so obvious Jessa felt foolish for not having thought of it herself.

Jessa borrowed the local phone book from the reference desk. The minute she turned to the *Woods* section her shoulders slumped.

"Look at them all. We can't phone all these people just in case someone had a great-grandfather called McDougall. There must be hundreds of them! Why couldn't he have been called Wyznicki? There's only one guy listed with that name."

"Try McDougall, then," Cheryl suggested. There weren't quite as many McDougalls, but still far too many to phone them all looking for distant relatives.

"So much for that," Jessa said. "Now what?"

Cheryl leaned back in her chair. "I don't know. Let me sleep on it."

"Speaking of sleep, I'm getting hungry."

The girls laughed. "Where are we supposed to meet Anthony?" Jessa asked.

"At the coffee shop down past the antique shop. We'd better go now. He'll be getting worried."

14

For the second morning in a row Jessa stopped, dumb-founded, in front of the K.M.S. School Spirit bulletin board. It seemed the poster about Andrew had sparked some competitive spirit in the other students. A hand-drawn poster with a rather good drawing of a leaping basketball player congratulated all the boys in Grade Nine who had made the basketball team. Each of their names was listed and beside each was a happy face drawn on a sticker of a basketball. Under that was an announcement encouraging runners to try out for the cross-country running team and a colourful poster put up by the drama club announcing auditions for an all-grade production of *A Midsummer Night's Dream*.

None of these posters was of any interest to Jessa. What caught her eye was a big poster of a sad-eyed little girl poking a syringe into her leg. Under the picture it said

INSULIN IS NOT A CURE
Support diabetes research by bringing in
your empty pop cans and bottles.

All proceeds will be donated to diabetes research.
Remember—diabetes isn't a disease just for old people.
Jessa Richardson, a student at K.M.S., is a diabetic.
This can happen to anyone!

Jessa reached out to tear the poster down just as Mr. Belwell came up behind her.

"What a great start to the year, don't you think?"

Jessa jerked her hand back. "Um. Yeah. Great."

"You must feel pretty special to have such supportive friends," he added.

"Yeah, I guess so." Jessa's cheeks burned. The principal didn't yet know most of the kids in Grade Seven. But he knew Jessa because she and her mother had made a special trip to the school before classes started so Mrs. Richardson could explain all about Jessa's diabetes.

"I guess you changed your mind about sharing your story with the other students. I'm proud of you," he said, giving her shoulder a quick pat. "Good for you."

"Thanks," Jessa mumbled and hurried off down the hall before he could say anything else.

"Did you see it?" she demanded when she spotted Cheryl at her locker. "Did you see what that pig Andrew did now?"

"Calm down. What do you mean?"

"And it's all your fault! You should never have told him about my diabetes! Never!"

"What are you talking about?"

"The poster about the bottle drive! With my name on it!"

"Oh, that. I saw it. That's a pretty dramatic picture. How do you know Andrew did it?"

"Who else would want to humiliate me in front of the whole entire school? I bet he just couldn't wait to take his revenge. Well, he found the perfect way to get back at me, didn't he?"

Cheryl started to say something just as the bell rang. "What?"

"Never mind. Just don't do anything dumb before you check with me. Where did I put my English notebook?" She pulled binders, a sweater, and a box of cookies out of her locker.

"Right there?"

The notebook was on top of the pile as plain as day. "Oh, right. That would be the one! You've got me all distracted."

"Well, excuse me. You're not the one whose life has been ruined. I'm going to get Andrew. He can't get away with doing this sort of thing."

"Jessa, don't—" But Jessa didn't wait to hear what her friend had to say.

At lunchtime, Jessa deliberately carried her tray to Andrew's table and sat down opposite him. She didn't start to eat her bowl of chicken soup but stared at him until he, too, stopped eating and looked back at her.

She wasn't sure what she expected him to do or even what, exactly, she was going to say to him. But nowhere in her wildest imaginings had she pictured what words actually came out of his mouth.

"I'm really sorry."

"What?" She caught herself and set her face in what she hoped was a tough, unforgiving expression. "Well, you should be."

He looked a little taken aback. "I mean, I know what it feels like. I'm sorry it happened to you, too." He picked up his dinner roll, pulled off a piece, and popped it in his mouth.

"So, if you know what it feels like, why did you do it?"

Jessa watched as his expression changed from one of compassion to one of total disbelief. "You don't think I made that poster, do you? I mean, just because you were low enough to do something like that doesn't mean I would."

Jessa fought the urge to throw her carrot sticks at his head and run away from the table. "I did not make the poster! And even if I had, I wouldn't apologize because it was a really nice poster and I think it's great you are such a good rider!"

The two of them glared at each other, each waiting for the other to back down and admit to the hideous crime of poster-making.

"I didn't do it," they said in unison and then, despite herself, Jessa laughed. Andrew was so surprised at that he dropped his bread, and that made Jessa laugh harder. She put her hand over her mouth and tried to stop breathing to squelch her giggles. Her eyes started to water. It wasn't easy to stop laughing once she had started, especially when, to her amazement, Andrew joined in.

Finally Andrew managed to gasp, "You really didn't make the poster?"

Jessa shook her head. "Neither did you?"

"No. I wouldn't do something like that." He suddenly looked really serious. "I know how dangerous it can be to be . . . different."

He looked down at his tray, suddenly very interested in his bowl of soup.

"I'm sorry about what happened at your other school," Jessa said. "But you know, I don't think it will be the same here. Way too many kids at K.M.S. ride. And Jeremy Digsby goes to school here. He's in Grade Nine. He's one of the best riders around."

"Jeremy Digsby goes to school here?"

Jessa nodded. "Do you know him?"

"Well, I've seen him at a couple of horse shows. I don't know him personally. He goes to school here? At K.M.S.? And nobody ever . . . I mean, do people know he rides?"

It was Jessa's turn to look surprised. "He's pretty famous around here. Everybody figures he's going to go to the Olympics one day."

Andrew dipped his bread into his soup.

"Jeremy's really, really nice," Jessa said. "I'll introduce you to him." She glanced around the cafeteria. "I don't see him in here right now, but you two should definitely meet."

"Thanks," Andrew said. "That would be great." The corners of his mouth twitched into a quick, shy smile.

Jessa suddenly felt a warm rush of generosity. "And you could always ride with me and Cheryl sometimes. It's a lot safer to be on the trail with other people, you know."

Andrew nodded.

"Where do you keep your horse, anyway?"

"When I knew I was going to change to K.M.S., we found a little barn near Arbutus Lane. We can't afford the board at the Equestrian Centre, but Arbutus Lane is only about a ten-minute ride along the trail from where Lester is staying. He seems pretty happy. I want to take some lessons there."

"You know, if you're going to do clinics and lessons and stuff at Arbutus Lane, half the kids at this school ride there. Okay, that's an exaggeration. But you couldn't have kept your riding a secret for long."

Andrew bit his bottom lip. "I guess I knew that. It's just . . . I didn't want the same thing to happen again, you know?"

Jessa nodded.

"If anyone gives you any trouble, you come and talk to me," a growly voice said from behind Jessa.

"Cheryl!"

They all laughed and Cheryl sat down beside Jessa.

"So, you two kids are talking to each other?"

"About the posters," Jessa said. "We didn't do it."

"I know that," Cheryl said, just a little smugly.

"So," Andrew said, "if we didn't put up those posters, who did?"

"Another mystery," Cheryl said. "First the pocket watch and now this! We should set up a detective agency. We already have our magnifying glasses."

"Don't mind her. Last week we were going to be world-renowned archaeologists. This week detectives. Next week astronauts."

Andrew grinned and slurped down a big spoonful of noodles. Jessa opened her carton of milk and glanced sideways at Cheryl. She had not felt this happy since school had started.

"What pocket watch?" Andrew asked.

The girls quickly filled him in on everything that had happened and how they wanted to find a way to locate any living relatives.

"Why don't you put an ad in the paper?" he asked. "I think the *Stuff Found* section of the classifieds is usually free. We once found this white kitten and we put the ad in for nothing."

"That's a great idea," Cheryl said.

"Did the owners come and get the kitten?" Jessa asked.

Andrew shook his head. "Nope. Nobody ever called. We still have her. She's huge now. We called her Blanche because she's pure white."

"Which reminds me," Cheryl said. "Do you guys want to work together on that French skit that's due next week? We could do a really cool project about a waiter and a lost Canadian girl who is trying to find her way to some exotic pet shop in Paris."

Jessa rolled her eyes but didn't argue. Cheryl's crazy ideas were often the ones that wound up getting her the best marks in class.

"Mais, oui!" Andrew said. "She could be looking to buy a cheval! And the waiter might just be one of the best riders in France who is supporting his Olympic dream by serving croissants and French coffee to tourists."

"Oh, yeah! And she could maybe get a riding lesson from him or something. Jessa, you could be the girl and you could wear your riding boots and hat for the skit. . . ."

Jessa just nodded. She could not believe that the quiet, nervous boy she had despised only a short time before was actually turning out to be almost as goofy as her nutty best friend. Between the two of them, they were going to come up with the craziest French skit K.M.S. had ever seen.

15

Do you know any of these people? Robert Nigel McDougall, Elizabeth McDougall, or Albert Woods? Please contact Jessa or Cheryl. . . .

Jessa leaned against the wall behind the gym and chewed on the end of her pencil. "That's still a lot of words."

"Take out the second *McDougall.* She would have changed her name when she married Albert Woods."

Jessa scratched out *McDougall* and changed the ad to read *Have you heard of Robert Nigel McDougall or Elizabeth and Albert Woods? Please call. . . .*

"Okay, that's . . . one, two, three . . . fourteen words. Plus we'll add one phone number."

"Put mine in," Cheryl said. "I really, really want to talk to the person if someone actually calls."

"Fine." Jessa added the phone number. "So, Anthony is going to take you downtown right now so you can pay for this?"

"He's probably waiting outside the front of the school as we speak. Hurry up."

"It's too bad we couldn't figure out a way to use the

free *Stuff Found* section."

"Like you said, why would anyone call if they had no idea the watch was missing in the first place?"

The girls had pooled their allowance and returned a huge bag of pop cans to the grocery store to scrape together enough money to pay for a classified ad in the newspaper.

"Okay. When I get to the newspaper office, I tell them to put the ad in on Sunday, right?"

Jessa nodded. "I think that's the day most people would read the ads. Or maybe Saturday, when they're looking for the garage sales."

Cheryl sighed. "Okay. We'll do Saturday. I sure hope this works. We don't have enough money to try again."

Jessa slid the ad and the money into an envelope and handed it to Cheryl. "Good luck!" She wondered if they were just wasting their time. What were the chances that anyone would read the ad and then take the trouble to call? Slim to none, Jessa decided, and watched her allowance disappear into Cheryl's backpack.

"Jessa?"

Romeo gave a soft *wuff* from where he lay on Jessa's feet. Jessa groaned and rolled over. She squinted at her alarm clock and fumbled to find her glasses.

"What's wrong?"

Her bedroom door swung open and her mother's head peeked around the corner.

"Do I have to go to school?" Jessa was completely confused. It was the right time to get up for school, but wasn't it—

"No, honey. It's Saturday. Sorry to wake you so early, but Cheryl said it was life or death and I had to wake you up to come to the phone."

127

"Cheryl?"

"I told her you would call back later, but she wouldn't hear of it."

"Cheryl is calling now? Does she know it's Saturday?"

Jessa could feel the comfortable fog of sleep dissipating with every passing moment. It was hopeless. She was going to get up, give Cheryl a piece of her mind, and then go back to bed, even though she knew she'd never be able to fall asleep again.

"Hello?" she said groggily when her mother handed her the cordless phone.

"Took you long enough!"

"Do you know what time it is? I'm sleeping."

"Well, wake up. Mr. Maloney phoned me."

Jessa had no idea whom Cheryl was talking about. "Mr. Maloney? And I should care, why?"

"Don't you remember Mr. Maloney?"

Jessa racked her brains. "The only Mr. Maloney I can think of was that new teacher at Kenwood Elementary last year. The one who worked part-time in the library and coached the soccer team."

"Bingo!"

"Why did he call you?"

"You'll never guess who his grandmother is."

"Save me the trouble. Who?"

"Anna Bledsoe."

"For a minute I thought you were going to say Elizabeth Woods."

"Nope. But Anna Bledsoe is alive and well and living in a nursing home."

"Cheryl, would you please get to the point?"

"And her *mother* was Elizabeth Woods." Cheryl let this point sink in. "Mr. Maloney saw the ad, recognized the names, and called right away. He was very apologetic when he realized how early it was. He got very excited when I told him about the watch."

"You told him already?" Jessa was wide awake now.

"That was the whole point of this, right? Anyway, he said he seemed to remember something about some relative and a cougar but he didn't really know the details. So, you know what he suggested?"

"What?"

"That we come with him this afternoon to the nursing home to ask Mrs. Bledsoe if she remembers more. Robert Nigel McDougall would have been her grandfather."

"Wow. That's amazing."

"Yeah. He said most of the family has stayed on Vancouver Island except for Mr. Maloney's brother, who moved to New York two years ago. Oohhh, I can't wait to go and talk to her. I wonder what she can tell us about the watch?"

"Oh, wait—what about my riding lesson?"

"That's why I called so early. Call Mrs. Bailey and see if you can ride this morning instead. I'm sure it will be fine. If you go down there soon, you'll still have time for stalls and a lesson and we can be ready to go with Mr. Maloney this afternoon."

Jessa groaned. She deliberately scheduled her Saturday rides as late in the day as possible so she didn't have to get up at ridiculous hours.

"Fine. Will you come and help me?"

There was silence at the other end of the phone.

"Cheryl?"

Cheryl groaned. "I was going to go back to bed, actually."

Jessa screeched into the phone, "You get your lazy butt down to the barn. I'll meet you there in an hour!"

Jessa pedalled her bike up the long gravel driveway at Dark

Creek Stables just as Molly led Rebel out of his paddock.

"Hi, Jessa."

Jessa kept going right past the younger girl, fuming. Cheryl's change of plans meant she wouldn't get a private lesson after all. Her bad temper worsened when she retrieved Jasmine from the field and led her to the cross-ties only to find Rebel already standing there as Molly tugged a brush through his thick mane.

"Rebel's getting fuzzy," Molly said.

Jessa manoeuvred Jasmine into the second set of cross-ties. Where was Cheryl? If she'd been on time, Billy Jack would be in front of Jasmine, not Rebel.

"Happens this time every year."

Molly looked up at Jessa's sharp tone and Jessa felt a twinge of guilt.

"You know . . ." Molly said, her voice shaky. "I never asked to ride Rebel. I . . . I just wanted riding lessons and Mrs. Bailey thought . . . and you're so big . . . and I could never ride Jasmine . . . and . . . and . . ."

Molly turned away and wiped her eyes with the back of her hand. Jessa took a step towards her.

"Good morning, girls!"

Jessa froze and Molly slipped around to Rebel's other side. Jessa heard a muffled sniffle.

"Good morning," Jessa mumbled.

Mrs. Bailey peered at Jessa from under the brim of her black hat.

"Jessa. We need to have a conversation."

Jessa swallowed hard and glanced over at Molly. What could Mrs. Bailey want? Had she heard the way she'd spoken to Molly? Molly was so short that only the top of her head was visible above Rebel's withers. Great clouds of dust rose as she whisked the dandy brush over the pony's coat. She was right—Rebel's winter coat was growing in.

"Jessa—I want you to be perfectly honest with me. How do you like riding Jasmine?"

Jessa met Mrs. Bailey's gaze. There was no point in lying. "I . . . she's a great horse."

"That's not what I asked you. Do you enjoy riding her?"

Jessa couldn't speak. Silently, she shook her head. Molly's dandy brush froze in mid-air over Rebel's back.

"Fair enough. Jessa, you have a decision to make. The way I see it, you must decide where you want to go with your riding."

To the top, Jessa thought. There was nothing to consider. She stared at the toes of her riding boots and realized they could do with a good cleaning.

"And then you need to figure out how to get there. You can either tough it out with Jasmine, or we can try to find another horse for you to ride. There is, of course, another option." Mrs. Bailey paused and looked over towards Molly. "You can go back to riding Rebel and we'll find Molly another pony."

Jessa's heart leapt. She wanted to run over to Rebel and kiss him on the nose.

"You are getting a bit big for him, but if you take it easy, you would be fine for another year."

Take it easy. That meant no serious jumping—a few cross-poles, if she was lucky.

Jasmine nudged Jessa's side. "Do you smell carrots?" Jessa asked the big mare, who had an uncanny ability to locate any pocket containing treats. Jessa reached out to touch Jasmine's neck, aware now that both Molly and Mrs. Bailey were watching her. She dropped her arm to her side and moved over to Rebel's head. He nickered softly and pushed his nose into her open hand. Jessa fished a piece of carrot out of her pocket and Rebel lipped it from her palm. Behind them, Jasmine stamped her foot.

"She's jealous," Molly said, her bottom lip quivering.

Jessa nodded and her own eyes filled with tears. She pressed her forehead to Rebel's and reached up to scratch his favourite spot behind his ears. Rebel sighed the way he always did. "You like this, don't you, Rebel?" she managed to say, shocked at how shaky her voice sounded. "You look after Molly," Jessa said, clearing her throat. It felt as if she'd swallowed a huge stone. "Teach her to ride the way you taught me."

Molly's face crumpled and tears splashed over her cheeks. Jessa squeezed her eyes shut and fought not to let herself cry, but the big sob inside her escaped. She buried her face in Rebel's neck and wept. On Rebel's other side, Molly bawled into his mane.

Mrs. Bailey squeezed Jessa's shoulder. "My, my, Jessa. Molly. Please! This pony is not going anywhere!"

Through her tears, Jessa realized how utterly ridiculous they must look, hanging on to Rebel, weeping. A strange half giggle fought its way out with Jessa's next sob and Mrs. Bailey chuckled. Jessa turned to see the older woman dabbing at the corner of her eye with a red and white kerchief.

"Honestly! We hardly have all day to mope about. Do you girls want a riding lesson or not?"

Sniffling and nodding, both girls got back to work.

"Did you bring carrots?" Jessa asked.

"An apple," Molly answered.

"That's okay," Jessa said. "Rebel likes apples, too."

"That seemed like a pretty good lesson, from what I saw," Cheryl said as the girls waited for Mr. Maloney to pick them up from Jessa's house.

Jessa nodded. "It was better, I guess. Much better than

the show, that's for sure. I wish I'd been able to ride that well last weekend."

"You'll get it. Jasmine's a great horse and you're a good rider."

Jessa smiled. "Thanks."

"You have to focus on your ultimate goal," Cheryl said.

"The national eventing team?"

"Exactly! Maybe not with Jasmine. Maybe not this year. But you'll get there if that's what you really want to do."

Jessa grinned. Cheryl sounded a lot like Mrs. Bailey.

"I know that. I just don't feel very organized, you know what I mean?"

Cheryl shook her head. "As a very organized person, I have no idea."

"Oh, right. You are the least organized person I know!"

Cheryl threw the back of her forearm against her forehead in mock horror. "Why, however can you say that?"

"I've seen your closet, remember?"

"Yes, well. I know a lot about organizational theory. You should make a list of your goals for this coming year. And then another, ultimate list that ends with 'Olympic gold medal.'"

Jessa suspected her friend was half joking but decided such a strategy had some merit. "Is that him?"

Mr. Maloney waved from a blue sedan.

"Looks like it. Let's go," Cheryl said. "Hi, Mr. Maloney!"

Jessa scooped up a bunch of flowers her mother had picked from the garden. As she hopped in the car, she carefully laid the chrysanthemums across her lap. She hoped Mrs. Bledsoe was going to like them.

16

Jessa and Cheryl followed Mr. Maloney down a long hallway at the Kenwood Home for Seniors. The polished floors gleamed. Handrails ran along either side of the hallway, which ended in a bright, sunny room filled with plants.

"Hello, Granny," Mr. Maloney said to a white-haired woman sitting at a table beside a large birdcage. Several canaries flitted back and forth when the visitors approached. "I'd like you to meet two young ladies who used to go to my school."

Jessa and Cheryl exchanged glances. It was strange to hear a grown man call someone 'Granny' and even stranger to hear him call Kenwood Elementary 'his school' as if he owned it.

"Good afternoon. A pleasure to meet you."

"Nice to meet you, too," Jessa said. "Here. These are for you." She passed Mrs. Bledsoe the flowers.

"Thank you, dear. They are beautiful!" Mrs. Bledsoe's whole face wrinkled up when she smiled. She looked up expectantly at Mr. Maloney. "You have never been very good with introductions."

"Oh, of course. This is Jessa Richardson and Cheryl Waters. They would like to ask you a few questions about your grandfather—Robert McDougall."

"Doing a school project, are you?" Mrs. Bledsoe put the flowers gently on the table.

"Um, no," Jessa said.

"We actually wanted to ask you a couple of questions about your grandfather because we think we might have found something that belonged to him."

"Is that so? Now what on earth could you have found of Grandfather McDougall's?"

Cheryl pulled the watch from her pocket and handed it to Mrs. Bledsoe. The old woman's hand curled around the watch, and as she held it her hand began to shake.

"Well, I'll be . . ." Her sharp, grey eyes darted from Jessa's face to Cheryl's. "Where in heaven's name did you find this?"

Cheryl explained how they had found the watch and then figured out whom it might have belonged to by checking the reference books at the library.

"Well, I'll be jiggered. This likely *was* my grandfather's watch. Do you know the story of what happened to him?" She didn't wait for the girls to answer. "He shot himself."

"Really? We thought he was attacked by a cougar."

"Well, you really have done your homework. You must have read one of the newspaper accounts. Those reporters only ever tell you half the story. There was a cougar, all right, but that wasn't what killed my grandfather."

"What happened?"

"Well, if you'd really like to know, why don't you girls sit down and make yourselves comfortable."

As Jessa pulled a chair closer and sat down, old Mrs. Bledsoe turned the watch over and over in her hands. She ran her thumb over the back cover and then pressed a tissue to her nose. When the girls were settled, she cleared her throat and began.

"My grandfather worked for the Dark Creek Railway Company. I never knew him, of course. The accident happened just before my mother was to be married."

Jessa nodded, thinking that at least the paper had been right on that account.

"Nineteen-eighteen was a bad year for cougars. Up near Lake Cowichan a boy and a girl were attacked by a cougar while they were out looking to catch their horses."

"Really? What happened?"

"They managed to beat the cougar off with their bridles, of all things."

"I guess the bits would be pretty heavy if you clunked a cougar on the head with one," Cheryl said.

"Yes, I suppose you are right about that." Mrs. Bledsoe smiled. "It was a miracle, but both those children survived. My grandfather, bless his soul, might have survived if he had stayed put and waited for help."

"What do you mean?"

"He was attacked not far from a storage shed out on the part of the Dark Creek Railway line near Kenwood. The cougar jumped him, but he was able to scare it away with a stick. He made it back to the shed where he had been working earlier and decided he had to protect other people in the area. He was loading his gun, intending, I suppose, to go off and shoot the cougar. Instead, he accidentally shot himself in the knee."

"Oh!" Jessa cried.

"In the shed?" Cheryl asked, aghast.

"That's where a work crew found him hours later. He had lost a lot of blood—some from the cougar attack, but even more from the gunshot wound. He developed blood poisoning and died about a week later. It was very, very sad. My mother was always broken-hearted that her father had not been at her wedding."

Everyone sat very quietly for a moment. Mrs. Bledsoe picked up the watch.

"Tell me—where on earth did you find this?"

"Under the shed," Cheryl said. "We were pretending to be archaeologists and that's what we found."

"Pretending? A genuine archaeologist couldn't have found anything more precious than this. I'm amazed that old shack is still standing!"

"I wonder if your grandfather dropped the watch that day he shot himself? It could easily have fallen through one of the cracks in the floor."

Mrs. Bledsoe brought the watch close to her face and squinted at it again. "I don't suppose we will ever know for certain what happened on that terrible day."

For a moment, the old woman seemed to drift off somewhere far away. Mr. Maloney caught Jessa's eye and inclined his head towards the long hallway.

"May I ask you one more question before we go?" Cheryl said.

Mrs. Bledsoe nodded.

"How, exactly, are you related to Mr. Maloney?"

"That's a simple question—this old brain can still remember the answer to that one quite easily. I married Blake Bledsoe in 1941, and about a year later we had a daughter, Fanny. She married Billy Maloney in 1965. They had four children including Kevin here. Kevin is one of my fourteen grandchildren."

Jessa willed herself not to laugh. It was just too strange to hear Mr. Maloney being called by his first name. She knew it was silly, but somehow she never thought of teachers having first names or grandmothers.

Mrs. Bledsoe took another long look at the watch and

then handed it back to Cheryl. "Thank you so very much for letting me see the watch. I can scarcely believe it even though I've seen it with my very own eyes."

Cheryl looked at Jessa, and without saying a word, Jessa nodded.

"Here, Mrs. Bledsoe." Cheryl handed the watch back. "You should really have this. It was just lucky we found it. It doesn't really belong to us."

"Oh, my—" Mrs. Bledsoe reached for another tissue. This time, a tear escaped and trickled down her cheek. "Bless you, my dears. What a sweet thing to do."

Mr. Maloney patted his grandmother's hand. "I'm so glad I read the paper this morning," he said.

"So am I, Kevin. So am I."

At lunch on Monday, Jessa joined a group of about ten kids all gathered around one of the big round tables in the cafeteria. Most of the faces were familiar—Cheryl, Midori, Rachel, and Monika—but there were some new faces too, including Andrew and a boy from Cheryl's drama class who had huge, poofy hair and a nose ring.

Jessa had just sat down when Rachel called out, "Hey, Jeremy! Come sit with us!"

Halfway across the cafeteria with his lunch tray, Jeremy changed directions and headed towards the big group. He laughed good-naturedly as everyone else at the table shifted around to make room for him.

"This is Andrew," Rachel said as if she had been the one to discover the new rider in their midst.

"Yes, I know."

Andrew looked surprised. "You know me?"

"Well, not exactly. Monika told me you'd been at the show and that you were going to school here now. How did you like my welcome poster?"

"*You* made the poster?" Cheryl said, nearly choking on a carrot stick.

"I recognized you in one of the photos my mom took at the show. I didn't need the picture so I thought I'd make a poster."

"It was kind of a surprise," Andrew said and then quickly added, "but thank you very much. I didn't know so many kids rode at this school." All things considered, Jessa thought, Andrew was being very gracious.

"Yeah—quite a few of us ride," Jeremy said with a grin.

"That was a great poster," Monika said. "Why doesn't anybody ever want to make one for me?"

"Because you're not special enough," quipped Rachel. "You have to be a fantastic rider and new to the school or have a dramatic disease, like Jessa."

Jessa winced. She had been hoping the conversation would change before it got around to the subject of Jessa's poster. Obviously, she was out of luck.

"Did you like the poster?" Midori asked.

Jessa was about to tell Midori and everyone else at the table exactly what she thought about the poster when Midori added, "I make my family join the march for diabetes so we can help you get better."

The penny dropped. *Midori* had made the poster—not to embarrass her at all, but because she really did want to help. Jessa swallowed. She didn't think she had ever felt like a bigger fool than she did right at that moment. She could not think of a single thing to say.

"Hey, when is that march, anyway?" Andrew asked.

"First weekend in October," Midori said.

"So we have time to get pledge forms and sign up sponsors and register. . . ."

"Great idea, Andrew," Cheryl chimed in. "Why don't

139

we all go as a big group? We could dress up and wear blood-coloured costumes. . . ."

"That's disgusting!" Rachel said. "The blood-coloured costumes, I mean. I think it would be fun to march, though."

"Oh, I know!" Cheryl said, bouncing up and down in her seat. "We could make orange cone-hats and go as syringes."

Everyone at the table burst out laughing. Despite herself, Jessa grinned right along with them. She decided that marching in a fund-raising parade wouldn't be so bad. In fact, she thought as she looked around the table, with this group of friends, it could be a most entertaining way to spend an afternoon.

Photo: Diane Morriss

About the Author

Nikki Tate lives in Victoria, British Columbia, and is a much sought after workshop leader who is entertaining, inspiring and informative. She enjoys working with young aspiring writers and has spoken to thousands of school-children across Canada about the writing process. All of Tate's novels have received consistently positive reviews and have appeared on the BC Bestseller list time after time.

Visit Nikki's website:
www.stablemates.net

Books by Nikki Tate
Available from Sono Nis Press

The StableMates Series

StableMates 1: *Rebel of Dark Creek*
StableMates 2: *Team Trouble at Dark Creek*
StableMates 3: *Jessa Be Nimble, Rebel Be Quick*
StableMates 4: *Sienna's Rescue*
StableMates 5: *Raven's Revenge*
StableMates 6: *Return to Skoki Lake*
StableMates 7: *Keeping Secrets at Dark Creek*

The Tarragon Island Series

Tarragon Island
No Cafés in Narnia

The Estorian Chronicles

Book One: *Cave of Departure*
Book Two: *The Battle for Carnillo* (coming in Fall of 2002)